THE GHOSTS OF EDEN HOLLOW

THE GHOSTS OF EDEN HOLLOW

Scott M. Baker

Also by Scott M. Baker

Novels
Nurse Alissa vs. the Zombies
Nurse Alissa vs. the Zombies: Escape
Nurse Alissa vs. the Zombies III: Firestorm
Nurse Alissa vs. the Zombies IV: Hunters
Nurse Alissa vs. the Zombies V: Desperate Mission
Nurse Alissa vs. the Zombies VI: Rescue
Shattered World I: Paris
Shattered World II: Russia
Shattered World III: China
Shattered World IV: Japan
Shattered World V: Hell
The Vampire Hunters
Vampyrnomicon
Dominion
Rotter World
Rotter Nation
Rotter Apocalypse
Yeitso

Novellas
Nazi Ghouls From Space
Twilight of the Living Dead
This Is Why We Can't Have Nice Things During the Zombie Apocalypse

Anthologies
Cruise of the Living Dead and other Stories
Incident on Ironstone Lane and Other Horror Stories
Crossroads in the Dark V: Beyond the Borders
Rejected for Content
Roots of a Beating Heart
The Zombie Road Fan Fiction Collection

A Schattenseite Book

The Ghosts of Eden Hollow
by Scott M. Baker.
Copyright © 2021. All Rights Reserved.
Print Edition
ISBN-13: 978-1-7351312-8-3

Cover Art © Warren Design

CHAPTER ONE

18 December 1945
Eden Hollow, Eden, Vermont

NICK THOMPSON STOOD by the window to his flat, staring out into the woods, a lit cigarette in his hand. He had not been smoking it, so a two-inch tube of ash dangled precariously from the tip. Not that he cared if the ash dropped and ruined the carpet. This place meant nothing to him anymore.

Ben and his wife Kathleen, an auburn-haired beauty, had moved in here as newlyweds a little over four years ago. Their life had been perfect for five months. Then the Japanese bombed Pearl Harbor and Nick, like millions of other patriotic Americans, joined the military. He had chosen the Navy like his father and grandfather before him. Kathleen stayed behind, volunteered at the local Red Cross station, and promised to write him every day.

Seven months later, Nick and his shipmates were getting their asses handed to them by the Imperial Japanese Navy at the Battle of Savo Island off Guadalcanal. He became one of a handful of survivors when the cruiser *U.S.S. Vincennes* was sunk after taking seventy-four hits from Japanese warships. Luck had been with him that night, as it would be for the rest of the war. Over the course of the next three years, he survived one more sinking and three *kamikaze* attacks, all without a scratch. He barely believed his luck three months ago when he stood on the deck of the battleship *Missouri* to witness the Japanese sign the terms of surrender ending World War II. Nick had survived against all odds.

True to her word, Kathleen had written him daily. Every few weeks, he would receive a batch of letters from her, which he read so frequently they nearly fell apart. Kathleen told him about wartime life in Eden and her volunteering with the Red Cross, how much she loved and missed him, and how she couldn't wait until they were together again. In many of the letters, she described in explicit detail how she would welcome him home. A few contained bad news, like the one in which she informed him his grandfather had passed away and willed his fortune to him. Whether good or bad, those letters had kept him going. They were the lifeline to his one true love. Reading them gave him the courage to deal with the death and destruction he witnessed all too frequently. When he lost them during a *kamikaze* attack in Leyte Gulf the previous October, it devastated him. Thankfully, a new batch arrived a week later.

With his tour of duty complete, the Navy discharged him. Nick could hardly contain himself. Rather than call Kathleen and tell her was coming home, he decided to surprise his wife. Several times on the trip home he had picked up the phone to tell her the news, always hanging up before he made the connection, wanting to see her reaction when he showed up at their flat.

Nick arrived last night. Only he was the one surprised. He entered the flat to find Kathleen in bed with another man. The son of a bitch, rather than be ashamed, attacked Nick for barging in on them. Because of his military training, Nick took him down quickly, breaking his jaw in the process. Nick wished he had broken his neck. Rather than come to her husband's defense, Kathleen went to the other man. When the police arrived ten minutes later, the bitch accompanied her lover to the hospital. Thankfully, the police refused to press charges, one of the officers telling him that if they prosecuted every returning serviceman who beat up their wives' lovers the jail would be packed.

That was twenty-four hours ago and Kathleen still had not

returned.

Some of the other tenants and the landlady filled him in that morning on what had been going on. The gigolo was Joel Hemmings, a 4-Fer who also volunteered at the Red Cross where he met Kathleen. They became good friends and, not long after that, took their relationship to an intimate level. The two had been lovers for more than three years, ironically spending their first night together at the same time the *Vincennes* was being shot out from under Nick. One of the female residents had tried talking to Kathleen about her affair and had been told to mind her own business. The landlady had considered writing to Nick about it but didn't want to place such a burden on him when there was nothing he could do about it. He appreciated their support.

Nick made the decision that afternoon to re-enlist. While he could overlook the indiscretions of a lonely wife, he could never forgive Kathleen for leaving him in his moment of heartbreak to be with her lover. A car would pick him up in the morning and drive his back to Boston.

The door to the flat opened and quietly closed. "Nick," Kathleen whispered.

He refused to look at her. "What do you want?"

"I want to talk."

"There's nothing to talk about."

"I want to explain what happened."

"Are you going to try to explain how you've been fucking another guy for over three years and went with him to the hospital rather than stay with me?" Nick raised the cigarette to his lips. The tube of spent ash dropped onto the carpet. He took a long drag and blew smoke onto the curtains. "You made your choice and I made mine."

"What do you mean?"

"I'm going back to the Navy. I'll start a new life for myself and you can be happy with Joel."

"I don't want to lose you."

"You should have thought about that three years ago."

"What about your inheritance from your grandfather?"

Nick felt the emotional knife Kathleen had plunged into his heart churn. The bitch didn't give a shit about him. She only cared about his money. He fought back tears and anger. "You'll never see a dime of that."

"I'll fight you for it in court."

He laughed derisively. "Good luck. Not many judges will look favorably on a cheating whore."

Kathleen gasped, party from anger and partly from the realization she had forfeited a fortune. A moment later, she sniffed back a tear. "I'm sorry."

"Too late for that now."

"I know something that will make it right."

"What?" Nick spun around to confront his wife.

He died a few seconds later.

CHAPTER TWO

The Present

*Y*OU GOT THIS, *girl.*

Tatyana Reynolds checked herself in the bathroom mirror. She had spent half an hour this morning going through her closet trying to find an outfit that blended college casual and business professional. The combination she chose was shiny black flats, a navy-blue skirt that stopped just above the knees, and a cream-colored blouse. For an added touch, she wrapped her shoulder-length blonde hair into a ponytail to make her appear slightly older than twenty-five. Tatyana gave herself a nod of approval. She needed to make a good first impression.

Leaving the bathroom, Tatyana made her way to the third floor where Doctor William Lasota had his office. As part of her PhD program, she needed to obtain a full-time internship to gain teaching experience if she hoped to find a position as a professor with another university upon graduation. Plus, she needed the money. Her bank account had dropped below a hundred dollars and the rent on her apartment was overdue. She had sold her car, a ten-year-old Subaru Forester, to make ends meet. If this internship didn't work out, she would have to pick up a full-time job which wouldn't pay much and would seriously cut into her study time. The college had arranged one with Doctor Lasota, pending his approval. She interviewed with him in five minutes.

Tatyana never had Doctor Lasota for a class, knowing him solely by his reputation. He was a stickler for details and a hard ass in the classroom. He assigned a lot of reading, his tests were notoriously difficult, and he demanded graduate-quality term papers. However, most of his students loved him. He brought history to life and immersed his lessons in whatever subjects were being covered, partly because he dressed in period costumes. Tatyana's one encounter with the doctor had been during her first year at Dartmouth when she saw him walking across campus dressed as a Franciscan monk to teach Medieval Studies. Getting this internship would be a huge check mark on her resume.

Standing in front of his office, Tatyana paused and took a deep breath to calm her jitters. *You got this, girl,* she told herself, repeating her usual mantra. She knocked on his door.

"Come in," answered the voice on the other side.

She stepped inside. "Doctor Lasota, I'm Tatyana Reynolds. I'm here to interview for the internship."

"Come in and shut the door," he said with a warm smile.

In his early thirties, Doctor Lasota was one of the youngest professors on campus. Tall and attractive, he exhumed a charming personality at odds with his reputation in the classroom. This would be easier than she thought.

"Have a seat." He pointed to the wooden chair beside his desk. "I love a person who's on time. It shows responsibility and that you're serious about this position."

"Thank you." Tatyana took the seat. "And I am serious about this internship."

Doctor Lasota spun his chair to face her and moved it closer.

Tatyana opened the cream-colored file folder she carried. "I brought you my resume to look over."

"No need for that. I already have one." He picked up a copy from his desk and scanned it. "I read through your academic record this morning. A 3.97 GPA at Colby College and a 3.93 GPA in your Masters' Program at Tufts. A member of Phi Kappa Phi and Phi Alpha Theta. It's impressive."

"Thank you, Dr. Lasota."

"Please, call me Bill."

"Okay."

"As I was saying, your academic record is outstanding." He tossed the resume on top of his desk. "This position is not your average internship where you'll teach a few classes and grade tests. I'll be taking you under my wing and preparing you for your PhD. That's a lot of work on my part. I need to make sure I'm taking on someone who is as fully dedicated to this as I am."

"I assure you, Doc... Bill... that I'm dedicated to getting my PhD. And to working with you."

"You realize this internship is a full-time position. Will you be able to handle this as well as your studies?"

"I know it won't be easy, but I'm more than willing to do what it takes."

"I'm glad to hear that. You know, there'll probably be a lot of late nights involved with this internship."

"I understand."

"Good." Doctor Lasota pushed his chair even closer to Tatyana and placed his right hand on her knee, his fingers playing with the hem of her skirt. "I think we have ourselves a deal then."

"Let me get this straight." Tatyana flashed Lasota a con-spiratorial smile. "You're saying the TA position is mine as long as I give you a little T and A on the side?"

"I wouldn't put it that way, but I think you understand what's expected of you."

"I do."

"Good." Lasota placed his left hand on Tatyana's other knee and pushed her legs open, spreading her skirt. "Then let's settle this arrange—"

Tatyana slammed her legs shut, her knees crushing the doctor's knuckles together. He yelped and removed his hands. "What the fuck? I told you the internship is yours if you want it."

"I do want it, but because I deserve it. Because I earned it. Not because I put out for you."

Lasota pushed his chair back over to his desk. "Miss Reynolds, it's time you pull your head out of that pretty little ass of yours and begin to realize this is how things work in the real world. It's not what you know, it's who you blow."

Tatyana could restrain her temper no longer. She stood so rapidly she tipped over her chair. Part of her wanted to slap the professor across his face. Another part wanted to kick him in the balls repeatedly and hard enough that it'd be a long time before he preyed on any more of his students. The worst part, Lasota could not have cared less about her anger, fixing on her a stare part pity for her wasted life and part contempt for her inability to play the game. Tatyana opted for the less violent response.

"I'd rather screw one of the dead at the campus morgue than you."

"Be my guest." Lasota turned his attention back to what he had been doing.

Tatyana seethed. She spun around and stormed across the room. As she placed her hand on the knob, Lasota spoke without raising his head. "While you're over at the medical school, you might want to consider transferring majors. Your academic career over here will not be pleasant."

Tatyana stepped into the hall and slammed the door behind her. Heading to the main exit, she hoped she would make it home before breaking down in tears.

CHAPTER THREE

TATYANA ALREADY HAD plans to meet her best friend, Julie DeFelice, for dinner at the Pine at the Hanover Inn, across from the Dartmouth Green, which turned out to be fortuitous considering how her day had gone.

She had met Julie during her first year as a grad student at Tufts and they became fast friends, which surprised a lot of people considering their personality differences. Julie was an outgoing person, to put it mildly. Both women were equally attractive, yet Julie always highlighted her good looks with heels, short skirts, and designer blouses with the two top buttons undone. While Tatyana spent her nights and weekends studying in her dorm room or at the library, Julie would hang out with friends, tutor other students, or spend time volunteering at the local animal shelter. And dating. It seemed as if every guy on campus had asked her out at Tufts. Not that Tatyana could blame them. To call Julie an extrovert would be an understatement. She had one of those vibrant, outgoing personalities that placed everyone at ease. She once made Doctor McAuliffe, one of the dowdiest professors in the History Department, burst out laughing at one of her jokes.

Tatyana could certainly use some uplifting tonight. The half-empty wine glass in front of her was proof alcohol wasn't doing the trick.

Julie arrived at ten minutes past the hour, habitually late and brimming with happiness. She searched the restaurant and, upon seeing Tatyana, broke into a huge smile and made her to her friend. Once at the table, Julie embraced Tatyana, who was still in her seat.

"It's so good to see you. How've you been?"

Tatyana hugged her friend. "I've had better days."

Julie slid into the seat opposite her friend. "I can see that by your sour expression and the glass of wine."

"This is my second glass."

"I take it your interview for the internship didn't go well?"

"That's putting it mildly." Tatyana drank some more wine.

"Slow down, girl. You'll be drunk way before I am."

"You know I don't like getting drunk."

"Maybe you should." Julie smiled at her friend then became serious. "What happened?"

"Long story short, Doctor Lasota wouldn't give me the position unless I assumed a few positions for him."

"Did you?"

"No!" Tatyana said it loud enough that several patrons turned to her. She felt her face flush with embarrassment and lowered her voice to a whisper. "You know I'm not that type."

"I'm teasing. Good for you, though. You're too talented to get ahead by putting out."

"I wish it were as simple as that. I needed that internship. Without it, I won't have the money or the experience to get my PhD."

The waitress passed by with a tray of food. Julie raised her hand to catch her attention. "When you get a moment, can I get two more glasses of wine?"

"I don't need any more wine," said Tatyana.

"Yes, you do." To the waitress, "Bring two glasses, please."

"Of course. Let me take care of the other table first."

"Thank you." When the waitress left, Julie leaned closer to her friend. "If you need a loan, maybe I can help."

"Thanks, but I doubt it."

"I'm doing well at my job. How much?"

"Ten thousand dollars."

"Wow. I'm not doing that well. Sorry."

Tatyana forced a smile. "That's okay. But I appreciate the offer. Even with a doctorate in history, I'll probably still wind up working at a Dunkin' Donuts somewhere."

"But with a PhD you'll be *managing* that Dunkin' Donuts."

Tatyana chuckled. Julie always knew how to cheer her up. Damn, it was good seeing her friend again.

The waitress came up with their glasses of wine and asked if they were ready. Tatyana ordered the salmon and rice. Julie opted for a Caesar salad with chicken. As the waitress thanked them and left, Julie turned her attention to Tatyana.

"Enough about Professor Pervert. What's been happening with you?"

The two women spent the next hour eating, drinking, and getting caught up on their lives since they last met. There was not much for Tatyana to relate. The life of a twenty-five-year-old college student who didn't party or date was boring. Julie had a different story. After grad school, she had moved to Connecticut and taken a job as a background investigator for Perspecta, conducting investigations on people seeking security clearances. The pay was good, she set her own hours, and got to travel at the company's expense, including a two-week training course in Colorado, which explained all those pictures of the Rocky Mountains she had posted on Facebook. The best part was uncovering people who tried to conceal the sordid details of their past. In a few years, she could be promoted to regional manager. Julie even had a steady boyfriend. Tatyana envied her friend's success.

"What brings you to Lebanon? Business?"

"You remember my grandmother?"

"Emelia?" asked Tatyana. "The one who lives in Vermont?"

"The same."

"I like her. She always tried to overfeed us."

Julie mimicked an Italian accent. "Men don't marry skinny women. They prefer a little meat on the bones."

Both women chuckled at the memory.

"It's her eightieth birthday this weekend and I'm going to see her. And you're coming along."

"I can't."

"Why? Do you have a date?"

Tatyana didn't want to admit that Doctor Lasota's inappropriate advance was the first time a guy had paid attention to her in three years. "I have a report to write."

"When is it due?"

"Next month."

Julie made a sound like a game show buzzer. "Wrong answer."

"I have classes to study for."

"You need to get away from here for a while. The mountain air will do you good."

"Well, I guess I could bring my textbooks with me."

Julie made the game show buzzer noise again. "Wrong again. If I see a textbook, I'll throw it into the fireplace."

"What will I do up there?"

"Relax. Take a hike in the mountains. Get some sun. Enjoy yourself."

"Three days without reading. I'll go nuts."

"Then bring a trashy romance novel. Get that libido going again."

"I don't know."

Julie had never been known for giving up without a fight. "Besides, Emelia says the house is haunted. It'll give you a chance to use those Necromancy skills you're always talking about."

"You mean Necroscope."

"What's the difference?"

"A Necromancer brings people back from death or extracts knowledge by brutally eviscerating corpses. They're associated with black magic and witchcraft. I'm a Necroscope. They only communicate with the dead. And I'm not that good at it. I can feel the presence of spirits but don't chat with them."

"Stop making excuses. You're coming with me."

"What about my studies?"

"Three days aren't going to change your life."

Tatyana had to admit Julie was right. The idea of getting away from the college for a few days and spending it with a close friend sounded appealing. It would give her a chance to clear her head.

"Okay, you win. When do we leave?"

"Right after I pay the check and we swing by your place to grab your things."

CHAPTER FOUR

THE WOMEN DIDN'T talk much on the two-hour ride to Emelia's place in Eden, Vermont, a few miles south of the Canadian border, which suited Tatyana fine. It gave her a chance to forget the unpleasantness of the day and enjoy the luxuriousness of her friend's midnight black Mercedes E-300. By the time they reached Emelia's mansion around nine o'clock, she was glad Julie had pressured her to come along. Tatyana looked forward to a quiet, relaxing weekend.

Pulling off the main road, they passed a weathered, wooden sign that read Welcome to Eden Hollow. They continued for a mile along the driveway until the mansion came into view. Maybe mansion was on overstatement. The house was a twelve-room, three-story, brick structure built in the Federal style of homes that dominated Salem, Massachusetts during the city's seafaring days. The only additions to the traditional box-like design were a three-story tower in the front left corner with bay windows on each level and topped by a turret, a widow's walk on the roof, and an open-front porch that stretched from the tower along the front façade and partially down the right side. Tatyana planned on spending a lot of time on that porch.

Emilia's father had bought and refurbished the house for her, his only child, in the 1960s as a wedding gift so Emelia and her husband, Frank, would have a head start in life. Unfortunately for the happy couple, Frank died less than a year later from a heart attack before they had children. Emelia never remarried and had been living alone in this house ever since. Except for the tragic history, Tatyana envied her. She would never live in a home so elegant unless she won the lottery.

There were no cars in the circular driveway in front of the house.

"Looks like we're the first ones to arrive," said Tatyana.

"We're the only ones. Emelia has no relatives besides me and all her friends have long since passed on."

"How does she manage on her own?"

"My grandmother has someone living with her who cooks, cleans, and does the shopping. I've been trying to convince her to sell the property and move closer to me but she refuses. Says this is where she's lived most of her life and where she'll die." Julie chuckled. "The woman is as stubborn as a Sicilian mule. Not that I blame her. Who wouldn't want to live like this?"

Julie parked her Mercedes by the front stairs. The women removed their suitcases from the trunk. Emelia met them at the door.

For a woman turning eighty, Emelia appeared much younger than her age. Though barely five feet in height, she stood tall in the doorway, with no walker or cane to help her. Her hair, white with age, had been coiffured into an attractive hairstyle and dyed with streaks of strawberry blonde. Wrinkles stretched around her mouth and crows' feet circled her eyes which disappeared when she smiled.

"Julie, I'm glad you made it."

Julie placed her luggage on the porch and embraced her grandmother. "I wouldn't miss this for anything."

Emelia turned to Tatyana. "Tatyana, it's so good to see you again. It's been so long since you've been here."

"Ten years." Tatyana hugged Emelia. "I'm surprised you remembered my name."

"The body may be old, but the mind is as sharp as ever." She tapped her temple with her right forefinger then stepped aside. "Come in and get out of the cold."

The women stepped into the entry hall. The interior was just as Tatyana remembered it, elegant and old-fashioned. A balustrade staircase with a polished mahogany railing ran up the left side of the main hall. The walls were painted mustard with an apple green trimming. Both the dining room on the right and the living room on the left were furnished with well-preserved antiques – plush-covered wingback chairs and sofas, cherry-wood furniture, and area rugs covering the hardwood floors. Ornately chiseled marble mantles adorned the fireplaces in each room, both of which contained a roaring fire. Candelabras and electric lamps from the 1930s and 40s provided the illumination.

"It hasn't changed a bit since I was last here."

"It never will," explained Julie. "My grandmother detests modern furniture."

"It's all crap. Made of particle board and ugly as a baboon's behind." Emelia closed the door and made her way to the living room. "Leave your bags here and come sit by the fire."

Tatyana placed her suitcase by the bottom of the stairs. She spotted a nautical rondel mirror hanging on the wall with four lit candles placed in front of it. Tatyana wanted to see what she looked like in the candlelight. Stepping over to it, she examined her reflection. The image was slightly distorted, the silver backing having eroded over the years. Tatyana was attractive, though even she had to admit her ponytail and glasses made her look like a librarian. If she had lived a hundred years ago, she would have made a good Jane Eyre. Now all she needed to do was find her Mister Rochester.

The reflection of another woman, an angry scowl on her face, momentarily appeared in the mirror, startling Tatyana. She spun around, expecting to see Julie behind her. No one was there. A cold chill shivered down her spine.

"Julie?" she called.

"In here with grandma," she replied from the living room. "Join us."

"Just a minute."

Tatyana checked the mirror again. Nothing. Okay, she needed to stop drinking wine or, better yet, needed to increase her intake. Shrugging off the apparition as part of her stress, she joined the other women in the living area.

"Are you okay?" asked Julie.

"Yeah." Tatyana took a seat beside her friend. "Just a bit stressed out."

"Tatyana was turned down for an internship," Julie explained to her grandmother.

"Poor thing. What happened?"

Tatyana forced a smile. "Let's just say he wanted me in a different position than the one I applied for."

Emilia huffed. "Men can be such cads. Not my Frank, though. He was a perfect gentleman."

"Thank you for inviting me," said Tatyana.

"My pleasure. I don't get many visitors."

"I know, Grandma," said Julie. "I hate that you're alone here."

"Gracious, I have plenty of company, dear."

As if on cue, the housekeeper entered the living room holding a tray with tea and snacks. She was of average height and looks, with a professional yet pleasant demeanor. Tatyana guessed her to be in her mid-forties. "Here you go, Mrs. DeFelice."

"Thank you, Annette."

Annette placed the tray on a coffee table between the three women.

Emelia cooed. "Biscotti?"

"I thought you'd enjoy it."

"You're so good to me." Emelia took Annette's hand and patted it, then turned her attention to the others. "Annette makes the best biscotti I've ever had. I swear she has Italian in her blood."

Annette blushed. "Thank you, ma'am. Will there be anything else?"

"We're good. Girls, does breakfast at eight sound okay?"
Julie nodded.

"It sounds wonderful," Tatyana replied.

"If you wouldn't mind bringing their suitcases to their rooms first," Emelia said to Annette.

"I'll do that right away." Annette turned to the two women. "It was a pleasure meeting you."

Tatyana, Julie, and Emelia spent the next hour by the fireplace drinking tea and chatting, most of it from the grandmother who reminisced about her past.

CHAPTER FIVE

TATYANA DIDN'T MAKE it up to her room until nearly eleven that evening, which wasn't that late. She had pulled several all-nighters in college, but not after being hit on by an over-sexed professor and driving for several hours. Her body told her to go to bed. Her OCD compelled her to unpack first. Not that it would take long considering she had packed light.

Like the rest of the house, the guest bedroom was decorated in an elegant Federal style. An American Drew poster bed made of cherry wood sat in front of the window, the radiator a few feet to the left, pinging out heat. A cherry wood Hepplewhite chest stood across from the foot of the bed by the door. On the outer wall facing the rear garden, a burgundy-colored, upholstered wingback chair sat at an angle to the window with an antique-looking lamp behind it. Tatyana looked forward to reading by the window.

Placing the suitcase on her bed, Tatyana unzipped it. She removed her underwear first, turned around, opened the top drawer of the dresser, and placed them inside. Rummaging through the suitcase, she picked up her spare jeans. However, when she turned back to the dresser, someone stood in the open doorway.

Tatyana cried out and dropped her jeans.

"I didn't mean to startle you," said the figure.

"You almost scared the shit out of me. I didn't even hear you come into the room."

"Sorry. I tend to do that. My name's Nick."

Nick didn't offer his hand. Tatyana concentrated instead on

how attractive he was. Nick stood just under six feet in height with a lean body but, judging by the way he filled out his shirt, he had a well-toned and muscular physique. She wished he wore a t-shirt rather than a tan naval uniform, which seemed odd to her. Nick bore chiseled features and close-cut, dark blonde hair. Tatyana pegged him as a ladies' man. What struck her most was his eyes, stunningly blue and piercing. as if he could see into her soul.

"I'm Tatyana." She crouched to pick her jeans off the floor.

"I know. You're Julie's friend."

"You know Julie?"

"I know of her."

Tatyana placed the rest of her cloths in the drawer and closed it quickly, hoping he did not notice the underwear. "I'm surprised to see anyone else here. Julie said we were the only visitors."

"You are."

Now Tatyana was confused. "Do you live here?"

"I used to."

A sense of uneasiness settled over her. She did not get any vibes that Nick posed a threat to her or was dangerous in any way. It seemed more like an awkwardness about him, as though he concealed a secret he refused to share with her.

"So, you just pop in now and then?" she asked jokingly.

"Once in a while." Nick smiled. "Emelia doesn't mind me dropping by."

"How long are you staying?"

"Not long." Nick's cool demeanor grew awkward, like a teenager talking to his crush. "To be honest, I only dropped by to meet you."

"Really?" Now Tatyana was intrigued.

"I sensed a kindred spirit. Somebody who has been be-trayed. I wanted to say hello and tell you I'm sorry. And... you know... if you need to talk."

Frustration filled Tatyana. "Don't get me going about today."

"It was awful that your professor tried to take advantage of you like that."

"He's definitely an ass…. How did you know about that? Did Julie tell you?"

Nick shifted uncomfortably. "I shouldn't have brought it up. Forgive me."

"No problem."

"I should get going and let you unpack."

"You're welcome to stay and chat."

"I'll let you get your rest. Besides, I've probably caused enough trouble already."

Tatyana turned around, removed her cosmetics bag, and tossed it on the bed. "You're no trouble. I like your company."

When she looked back at the doorway, Nick was gone. When she rushed to the hall to tell him to come back, she could not see him anywhere, although she still sensed his presence. The man was either quick and quiet or the house concealed a secret passage, which wouldn't surprise her one bit. Eden Hollow was full of mystery. And she loved it.

"Come back soon."

Though Nick did not answer, she knew he would.

Closing the door, she moved over to the bed. She should take the time to wash off her makeup but was too tired. God knows it wouldn't be the first time. As she stripped out of her clothes and bra, a part of her wondered if Nick had snuck into a crawl space between the walls to watch her undress, immediately dismissing the idea. Nick did not seem like a pervert. As she slipped on her nightgown, the one she had worn for years with a cartoon image of a woman sitting in front of a pile of books with a glass of Merlot and the words "All I need is books and wine," she hoped Nick wasn't watching. He'd peg her as a nerdy girl.

Pulling the comforter and sheets aside, she slid under them and covered up. This bed was way more comfortable then her own. And with the radiator a few feet away, clanging out its heat, she felt comfy. She looked forward to a good night's sleep.

Just as Tatyana started to drop off, a cold chill washed over her, accompanied by a feeling of malevolence. She opened her eyes with a start and quickly switched on the light on her nightstand, fearful of what she would find. Nothing was there. The heat returned but the essence of evil still lingered.

"Is anyone there?"

Silence. Thank God.

Tatyana waited a minute before slipping back under the covers, although this time she slept with the light on.

There were a lot of mysteries about Eden Hollow yet to discover.

CHAPTER SIX

TATYANA ROSE AT seven thirty. She had slept fitfully, waking up several times and sensing the same malevolence she felt last night, even though nothing was in her room.

She quickly showered, put on makeup, and dressed. As she made her way downstairs, she had a lot of questions she wanted to ask Emelia.

Julie and her grandmother were already seated at the dining room table when she joined them.

Emelia burst into a smile. "Good morning, dear."

"Good morning. I hope I'm not late."

"You're just in time. Punctuality is something men admire in a woman."

"She's referring to me," said Julie.

"Nonsense. You're a good girl."

"Thanks."

"So, Tatyana. I hope you slept well."

"The guest room is wonderful. But I didn't sleep all that well."

"Same here," added Julie. "I felt like something watched me all night. Something evil."

"I'm sorry. That often happens when people come to visit. I'll have Annette light sage in your rooms. That should help."

"Please," began Tatyana. "Don't go to any trouble."

"It's no trouble at all, dear."

Annette entered, pushing a serving cart in front of her. She placed in front of each woman a plate of French toast and sliced strawberries, a dish of raspberry yogurt, and a cup of tea.

After putting down the pot of tea, two gravy boats filled with maple syrup and honey, plus small bowls with milk, sugar, and butter, she stepped back from the table.

"Will there by anything else?"

"Yes. Could you light some sage in the guest bedrooms, please?"

"Of course. I'll light some in every room as well."

"Thank you."

Annette pushed the serving cart back into the kitchen.

Tatyana poured syrup and honey on her toast and took a bite. "Oh, my God. This is delicious."

Emelia smiled. "I'll be sure to tell Annette."

"Usually all I have for breakfast is a bowl of cold cereal."

Julie chuckled. "I usually skip breakfast."

"That's not good," Emelia chastised lovingly. "Breakfast is the most important meal of the day. Besides, what have I always told you?"

"I know, grandma. Men like meat on their women."

"Speaking of men," Tatyana broke in with an awkward transition, "is anyone else staying here this weekend?"

"No, dear. Why do you ask?"

"Because a man stopped by my room last night to say hello."

"Was he dressed in a Navy uniform?"

"Yes."

Emelia waved her hand. "Oh, that's Nick. He pops in and out all the time. I enjoy chatting with him."

"You let a stranger come and go as he pleases?" asked Julie.

"Heaven forbid. Nick is one of the ghosts who lives here."

Tatyana and Julie looked at each other and then at Emelia.

"*One* of the ghosts?" Julie seemed dumbfounded.

"Yes. There are several, though most keep to themselves. I rarely see them. Nick is nice. He protects me from Kathleen."

Tatyana was intrigued. "Who's Kathleen?"

"Nick's wife. She's the mean one. She hates women. Kathleen is probably the reason you didn't sleep well last night."

Tatyana tapped Julie on the arm. "Did you know about this?"

"I knew the house had ghosts, but this is the first time I've heard any of the details." Julie turned to her grandmother. "Why didn't you tell me all this before?"

"You never asked, dear. Besides, I knew you wouldn't approve."

"You're damn right I don't approve."

Emelia wagged a finger at Julie. "Watch your language."

"Grandma, for God's sake, you're living in a haunted house."

"Haunted is such a misused word, dear. They're people who used to live here and for some reason never left. They share the house with me. I don't bother them and they leave me alone. Except for Nick. We're friends."

For Tatyana, everything now made sense. The apparition in the mirror last night. Nick's mysterious arrival and departure from her room. The malevolence she had sensed all evening. She had been picking up on the spirits' auras and had not even realized it.

Tatyana closed her eyes and cleared her mind, concentrating on the spirits who inhabited the mansion. She detected several auras, six or possibly seven, each a frightened soul who avoided interacting with her. Not because they feared her. They were terrified of another entity in the house, one that frightened them into submission. One of those entities, whose soul was pure and innocent, attempted to contact Tatyana, only to have her efforts thwarted by the others. Nick's aura came through the loudest, warning Tatyana of grave danger and promising her as much protection as possible.

Beneath it all, another spirit, dark and evil, threatened Tatyana if she stayed.

CHAPTER SEVEN

AFTER A TENSE and uncomfortable breakfast, Tatyana waited until Emelia had left to go about her daily routine.

"Julie, can I borrow your car to go into town?"

"What for?"

"I want to check out the library and find out everything I can about Eden Hollow."

"I'll drive you. I need to get out of here for a little while."

The closest library was the Lanphier Memorial Library, less than ten miles away. Half an hour later, the women parked in the town square and made their way inside.

It was a small, one-story, brick structure on Main Street. Entering the building, they approached the woman at the front desk, an attractive and slightly overweight middle-aged woman with pink-framed glasses and her brunette hair cut into a bob. Her name plate bore the name Michelle. She glanced up at them and smiled.

"Can I help you?"

"Yes, please. I'm looking for any information you have on Eden Hollow."

"Which one are you?"

Tatyana was confused. "I don't understand."

"Are you a journalist, a ghost hunter, or a thrill seeker. They're the only ones who ask for those files."

"We're none of those."

"I'm Julie, Emelia DeFelice's granddaughter. We're staying at the house and wanted to learn the history behind it."

Michelle's expression brightened. "I've heard of you.

You're the only heir to the estate."

"That's a cheery thought," huffed Julie.

"I can help."

Julie touched her friend on the forearm. "You're on your own with this. I'm going to find a coffee shop and have a few lattes."

"Fair enough. I'll find you when I'm done."

As Julie left, Michelle turned to the other woman behind the counter. "Darlene, can you watch the front desk for a few minutes?"

"Of course."

Michelle came around to Julie. "Follow me, please."

The two women made their way to the rear of the library.

"Excuse my being rude. Miss DeFelice is a lovely woman and a patron of the library. A lot of people come nosing around here looking for a story. I try to respect her privacy."

"I appreciate that."

Michelle stopped by a door with the word ARCHIVES painted on the glass panel. She unlocked it, switched on the lights, and pointed to a conference table in the center of the room.

"Have a seat, please."

Tatyana slid off her jacket, draped it over one of the chairs, and took the chair at the head of the table. Michelle stepped over to the shelves and removed a large book from the center, brought it over to Tatyana, and placed it in front of her.

"Over the years, I've compiled a collection of newspaper articles about Eden Hollow and placed them in this scrapbook. It's a lot easier than combing through the library's collection every time. Everything you need to know about the mansion's history is in here."

"You keep the book locked up?"

"It helps ensure Miss DeFelice's privacy. When you're done, leave the book on the table, lock the door behind you, and see me or Darlene on the way out. The phone on the wall connects with the front desk if you need anything."

"Thank you so much."

"My pleasure." Michelle left.

Tatyana opened the scrapbook.

Michelle had done an excellent job in pulling together various newspaper articles and local documents that detailed the history of Eden Hollow. According to the archives, the mansion had been built in 1819 by Bernard Wells, one of Salem's prominent merchants, as a retirement home for him and his wife Donna. They moved in the following year. Their happy life together was cut short in 1821 when Bernard accompanied one of his sailing ships to Asia to purchase chinaware in Shanghai and spices in the East Indies. The ship was lost at sea with all hands. In 1823, Donna Wells committed suicide by jumping off the widow's walk.

Possible ghost number one.

Since the Wells had no children, the mansion remained vacant until 1903 when a distant relative in San Francisco donated the property to the town of Eden. A developer purchased it a few years later and renovated it into a boarding house. One article reported that a speakeasy existed in the basement during Prohibition and that a young woman may have been murdered in one of the rooms. Naturally, with everyone worried about getting into trouble with the Feds, the story was covered up. Despite the lack of evidence, it remained a prominent but unsubstantiated rumor.

Possible ghost number two.

A fire broke out in the boarding house in 1923, killing four residents – a family of three on the second floor and a young man who witnesses claimed went back in to rescue them. The family had moved in less than a week prior to the fire and no records existed for them. The young hero was reported as one Kevin Dobbs, a wounded vet from The Great War. Only two bodies were retrieved.

Possible ghost three through six.

The mansion was repaired and opened again as a boarding house in 1926. No further incidents were reported until December 1945 when a brutal murder occurred. Tatyana read the report from the *Montpelier Evening Argus*.

2 January 1946 – Eden's peace and tranquility was shattered last week when a violent murder and assault took place at the Eden Hollow boarding house.

Ensign Nick Thompson, who had just returned home after spending three years in the Pacific, was violently murdered by his wife, Kathleen. Her motive for committing the gruesome crime has not been determined.

Residents of the boarding house who went to Thompson's defense were also attacked by Kathleen. Two injuries were reported, one severe. They were both treated at Copley Hospital. One victim is recovering from his wounds and is listed in stable condition. Both the police and hospital staff have declined to release the victims' names.

Following the attacks, Kathleen was shot by a resident of the boarding house. She was dead when the police arrived on the scene.

The incident took place in Room 12. Beyond that, authorities have refused to release any information about the crime. Attempts to obtain eyewitness accounts have been unsuccessful.

That confirmed Nick was ghost seven and Kathleen more than likely the malevolent entity.

The boarding house closed in 1947 after every resident refused to spend more than a few months in the residence, every one of them claiming an evil presence haunted the premises. The mansion remained vacant until Emelia purchased and refurbished the property in 1969.

And now Tatyana had become part of the story.

She went back to the article from *Montpelier Evening Argus* and scanned to the last paragraph where it stated Nick's murder took place in Room 12. She thumbed through the scrapbook, searching for a floorplan of the boarding house. She found one on the next to last page along with a newspaper article showing photos of the interior of the mansion before and after renovation. Room 12 was the last room on the right on the third floor.

The guestroom where she was staying.

That explained a lot.

Closing the book and grabbing her jacket, Tatyana left the archive room, locking the door behind her. She stopped at the front desk on her way out.

"Is Michelle around?" she asked Darlene.

"I'm sorry. She went to lunch. Can I help you?"

"I wanted to let you know I'm done."

"Thanks. I'll put the book away later. Did you find everything you were looking for?"

"Yes, thank you. Way more information than I expected."

"I'm glad. Have a good day."

Tatyana found Julie at a small mom-and-pop coffee shop across from the library. She slid into the booth opposite her friend.

"What did you discover?" asked Julie.

Tatyana spent the next few minutes relating everything she had read in the scrapbook. Though somewhat disinterested in the beginning, Julie's attention piqued when Tatyana told her the mansion's history as a boarding house, especially the murder of Nick.

"Do you think that's the same Nick who visited you last night?"

"It has to be."

"Wow." Julie broke the top of a cranberry muffin in half and offered some to her friend.

Tatyana waved her hand. "No, thanks."

"What next?"

"Did you bring a laptop with you?"

"I have an iPad."

"Can I borrow it?"

"Sure." Julie slid a chunk of muffin into her mouth. "What do you need it for?"

"I want to research how to ghost hunt."

CHAPTER EIGHT

THE CONVERSATION OVER dinner was a bit contrived, Tatyana wanting to avoid the topic of hauntings. She asked Emelia about how she furnished the house so eloquently and heard a long and fascinating tale about antique hunting throughout New England. Dinner provided another topic of conversation – clam chowder, lobster and scallop pie, and chocolate cheesecake, all made by Annette. The women finished off a bottle of zinfandel with dinner and nursed along a pleasant burgundy with dessert.

When finished, they moved to the sitting room, taking the half-finished bottle of wine with them.

"Dinner was delicious," offered Tatyana. "Do you always eat this good?"

"God, no." Emelia chuckled. "Most nights we have spaghetti or chicken. Tonight was a special occasion. I don't often have visitors."

Julie leaned back in her seat and patted her stomach. "I'll have to go the gym every day next week."

Emelia wagged a finger at her. "What have I always told you, dear?"

"Men like women with a little meat on their bones," Tatyana and Julie said in unison, enjoying a laugh.

Emelia winked at her granddaughter. "Your friend is a wise woman. And curious."

"What do you mean?" asked Tatyana.

"Michelle from the library called and mentioned you stopped by to do some research on Eden Hollow."

Tatyana's heart sank. "I'm so sorry. I hope you're not mad at me."

"Nonsense, dear. I'm pleased you showed an interest. And don't be upset with Michelle. She lets me know whenever anyone drops by looking for information about the mansion. She does it as a courtesy so I'm not bothered by outsiders."

"How often does it happen?" asked Julie.

"Not that often. I get a letter or phone call from someone three or four times a year asking if they could visit to talk with the ghosts. They're usually psychics or those curious about the afterlife. Occasionally I'm asked by writers if they could spend the night as research for one of their books. They're a pesty bunch. Once, I was contacted by one of those television ghost hunter crews."

"Did you let them in?"

"No." Emelia made a face that elicited a laugh from the girls. "They're all bullshit artists. I love when they go to a 15th century castle in Germany and talk to the ghosts in English. I was born at night, but not last night. Though I do enjoy the show with that pretty redhead and the detective from New York. I think they're legitimate."

Julie poured herself some wine and refilled Tatyana's glass. "You don't mind living with spirits?"

"Not at all. They don't bother me. Most of them keep to themselves. And as I said yesterday, Nick is nice to me. He checks in every now and then to see how I'm doing. Such a polite young man." Emelia rose from her chair. "Now, if you'll excuse me, I'm heading up to my room. I usually read for an hour before I go to sleep. See you in the morning."

After Emelia went upstairs, Julie leaned closer to Tatyana. "To be honest, it gives me the creeps sleeping in a haunted house."

"Not me. I find it exciting. It gives me a chance to use my psychic ability."

Annette entered the sitting room. "Can I get you ladies

anything?"

"Would I be a bother if I asked for a pot of tea to bring to my room?" asked Tatyana. "I'd like something to drink while I read."

"It's no trouble at all. I'll bring it up to you."

"Thank you."

The girls chatted for a few minutes then made their way upstairs, Tatyana stopping by Julie's room to pick up her iPad. When she entered her own room, a tray with a teapot and cup and saucer sat on the bed. A sage candle burned on the bureau, wafting a pleasant aroma through the room. Tatyana closed the door, kicked off her shoes, and brought the tray and iPad over to the easy chair where she made herself comfortable.

Turning on the iPad, she called up Google and typed in "ghosts." That term proved way too broad. She got hits for movies, TV shows, books, and dozens of other sites that defined what a ghost is or debated their existence. "Hauntings" did not fare much better, producing numerous lists of the most haunted locations in each state and major city. Typing in "how to get rid of" brought up a list of nuisances from fruit flies to stink bugs. Adding "ghosts" narrowed the search, although the most visited sites involved how to remove unwanted spirits from a host of video games.

Thankfully, farther down the list were tips on how to cleanse your property of spirits, although most of those were from newspapers and paranormal chat groups and were basic. They advised using sage, white candles, salt, white roses which suck spiritual activity out of the house, and crystals. Other advice offered was to ignore the ghosts so they would get bored and leave or tell them to leave because they were not wanted, though she doubted either of those would be effective. She needed a better search term.

This time, Tatyana entered the word "spectral" and several predictive texts popped up, including "spectral cleansing." Great. Page after page of detox supplements and procedures for colon enemas. Nope. She replaced "cleansing" with "exorcism" and still came up with nothing useful, although she did find an exorcist who would expel your demons online. Yeah, but no.

She had been researching for close to two hours and came up with nothing useful. She would have been better off reading a trashy romance novel.

Tatyana decided to check her email and social media before calling it a night. She typed in the userID and password into Google and, as her account came up, poured herself another cup of tea.

A child's voice said, "Hello."

CHAPTER NINE

TATYANA LIFTED HER head, surprised by the visitor.

A young girl approximately eleven years old sat on the edge of the bed, her feet dangling above the floor. She wore a dulled white nightgown that extended almost to her ankles. Long, unkempt brunette hair fell over her shoulders and down her chest and back, accentuating her emerald green eyes. Tatyana knew she belonged to the netherworld. She could sense the girl's spiritual aura, could hear her calling out from beyond the grave. However, like with Nick last night, this ghost had chosen to manifest itself in physical form rather than contact her telepathically.

The girl made eye contact with Tatyana, then focused her gaze on her feet, which she began back kicking against the mattress.

"Hello," said Tatyana.

"Am I bothering you?" she asked cautiously.

"Not at all, hon. I'm Tatyana."

"I know." The girl raised her head, making eye contact for a brief second. "I'm Gabriella."

"That's a beautiful name."

The girl smiled. "I'm named after my grandmother in Sicily."

Tatyana broached the next subject carefully. "I assume you're the girl who died in the boarding house fire?"

Gabriella closed her eyes and nodded.

"I'm sorry," said Tatyana.

"It's not your fault."

"I know. But I can still feel bad that it happened."

"Thank you." Gabriella lowered her gaze toward the rug. "You're nice, like that nice man down the hall who tried to help us. It was a horrible death."

"I can imagine."

"No. You can't." The girl did not say it to be demeaning or sarcastic but meant it as a statement of fact.

An awkward pause followed before Tatyana asked, "Why did come to my room?"

"I wanted to see if you were as nice as Nick says you are."

"Am I?"

"Yes." A shy smile pierced Gabriella's lip. "I haven't talked to anyone in so long."

"Are you shy?"

"Yes, but that's not the reason." Gabriella glanced around the room as if to make certain they were alone, then leaned forward and whispered. "She won't let us."

"Who?"

"Kathleen."

"Nick's wife?"

"Kathleen is mean. She won't let us talk to anyone who's alive, even Emelia. We're all afraid of her. Except for Nick."

"Why isn't Nick afraid of her?"

Gabriella shrugged. "He hates Kathleen for what she did to him but made a deal with her. If she leaves us and Emelia alone, he promised to forgive her. It's worked so far. But we're still scared and lonely."

"How many of you are there?"

"Eight in total." Gabriella began to count on her fingers. "Me and my parents. Mr. Dobbs, who tried to save us. Nick and Kathleen. Cheryl, who was killed in the basement. And Mrs. Wells, who jumped off the roof after her husband died."

"And the seven of you can't stand up to Kathleen?"

Gabriella shook her head fiercely. "She's not right."

"How so?"

Before the girl could answer, an icy chill washed through the bedroom. Tatyana shivered. The cold terrified Gabriella who jumped off the bed. Her eyes darted around the room.

"I have to go. I've already said too much."

"You can stay. You're safe with me."

"No, I'm not." Panic overtook the girl. "And neither are you."

A howl echoed from the hall outside. For a moment, it sounded like wind blowing through the mansion. Then the noise grew more guttural and terrifying.

"I'm sorry. Please don't hurt me." Gabriella ran for the closed door and passed through.

Tatyana raced over and whipped it open, searching the hall. Like Nick had done last night, Gabriella had disappeared without a trace.

A mist floated up the stairs and floated over the landing, then swirled down the hall toward Tatyana. As it approached, the mist changed. Arms, legs, and a head took shape, becoming more defined. The closer it got, the colder the hall became, plunging twenty degrees in seconds. When thirty feet away, the mist morphed into an apparition, taking the definitive form of an attractive woman adorned in a 1940s-style dress and shoes, but transparent. It picked up speed, jaunting down the hall.

Tatyana backed up, slamming her back into the jamb. The spirit quickened its pace. Tatyana moved into the bedroom, her eyes never leaving the apparition. Once inside, she grabbed the inner doorknob as the ghost centered itself in the doorway. Her face changed, the features of the young woman fading away into something almost demonic. Its mouth distorted into a twisted, angry grin with shriveled lips and jagged teeth. Its eyes morphed from blue to a deep crimson that seemed to glow in the dark. Its lids narrowed, focusing their glare on Tatyana, and its nostrils flared. When the spirit opened its mouth to speak, a biting cold and putrefying stench washed over Tatyana, making her eyes water and her stomach churn.

"You do not belong here!" Kathleen's voice was deep, guttural, and dripped with hatred. "Leave! Now!"

Tatyana slammed the door. When the wood struck the spirit, its form dissolved back into mist and floated away. The biting cold and stench dissipated, being replaced by the heat from the radiator and the aroma of burning sage.

Rushing over to the wing-backed chair, Tatyana sat down and took a long sip of tea to steady her nerves. It would be a good ten minutes before her heart rate returned to normal.

CHAPTER TEN

A HEAVY KNOCKING woke Tatyana. She bolted upright out of the wing-backed chair, half expecting to see Kathleen attacking her. The room was empty. Sunlight streamed through the windows. She had remained awake for several hours following the incident last evening and must have eventually dozed off in the chair. The knocking sounded again.

"Tatyana, it's Julie. Is everything okay?"

"It's unlocked."

Julie opened the door and peered into the room. She scanned the bed that had not been slept in and her friend. "Did you get any sleep last night?"

"Barely. You know Kathleen?"

"The malevolent spirit?"

"She came after me last night."

Julie rushed over to Tatyana. "Are you hurt?"

"Just scared. She told me to leave this place because I'm not wanted here."

"We'll be doing that right after breakfast. I have to get home early and get ready for a teleconference Monday morning."

"That's not all. Gabriella, the little girl who died in the fire, also visited me. She said the other spirits are afraid of Kathleen. Nick keeps the peace around here."

"Ghost drama," Julie chuckled. "It sounds like a reality TV show."

"It's not funny. I'm worried."

"I didn't mean to make light of it."

"I'm afraid I upset things."

"Even if you did, which I doubt, once we're gone every-thing should return to normal. Now come downstairs. Breakfast is ready."

✕ ✕ ✕

ANNETTE HAD SERVED strawberry yogurt, scrambled eggs and sausage, and slices of fresh melon and pineapple. The conversation was lighthearted, Tatyana avoiding any discussion about what had transpired last evening so as not to worry Emelia. Unfortunately, the talk centered around Tatyana's future, which only reminded her of the dilemma she faced once she returned home.

"I'm sorry to hear about things not working out with your internship," Emelia said with all sincerity. "I know you don't want to hear this, but it's probably for the better."

"I know," replied Tatyana. "It's just things are tough right now financially."

"As my mother used to say, and as I tell Julie all the time, one door closes so another one can open. You only need find it. God takes care of decent people, and you're one of them."

"Thank you. That means a lot." Tatyana didn't mention she was not religious. She hadn't attended church since high school.

"When are you girls leaving?"

"Right after breakfast," Julie answered. "I have to drop Tatyana off at college and then drive home. Next week is busy for me."

"I understand. I hate to see you go. I've enjoyed your company."

"It's been a lovely weekend," said Tatyana. "Thank you for having me."

"You're welcome, my dear. Please come back anytime." Emelia rose from her chair. "I won't delay you any longer.

Annette will clean up here. Please don't leave without saying goodbye."

"We won't, grandma."

Twenty minutes later, the girls were back in their rooms getting ready to depart, not that Tatyana had much to pack. She didn't even change, opting to take a shower once she got home. After dropping her clothes into the suitcase, she went into the bathroom and gathered her toiletries. When she stepped back into the bedroom, Nick sat in the wing-backed chair.

"Am I still welcome?"

"You are." Tatyana dropped her cosmetics bag into the suitcase. "Your wife isn't."

"I'm sorry about that. She's...." Nick sought the correct word.

"Nuts?"

"That about sums it up."

"No offense, but what did you ever see in her?"

"Kathleen wasn't like that when I married her." Nick pushed himself out of the chair and walked over to Tatyana. "As cliché as it sounds, she was one of the nicest people I've ever known when we got married. We were in love. Kathleen wrote me every day while I was overseas. I never expected to come home and find her in that bed with another man. Naturally, I was furious. I overreacted and sent him to the hospital. Kathleen got mad at me and went with him."

"Don't blame yourself for that. Anybody in your position would have a right to be pissed."

"As much as it broke my heart, I could understand her being lonely and finding someone else while I was gone. A lot of the guys I served with got Dear John letters. And a lot of them weren't faithful during ports of call. That's not why she killed me."

"What did you fight about?"

Nick sighed. "Even though she obviously cared more for

him than me, Kathleen didn't want a divorce."

"Maybe that means she still loved you."

Nick shook his head. "She loved my money."

"I don't understand."

"My grandfather passed away while I was in the Pacific and left me a little over two hundred thousand dollars. When I told Kathleen that I planned on leaving her and she wouldn't see a dime of the money, she killed me."

"What caused her to change?"

"Honestly, I have no idea. The Kathleen I came back to was not the same woman I left. She's...." Again, Nick searched for the right word.

"Evil?" offered Tatyana.

Nick lowered his head and nodded.

"Is everything Gabriella told me about her accurate?"

"Yeah. She's terrorized the other spirits into submission. The only reason Kathleen leaves Emelia alone is because I agreed to stay with her rather than travel on into the afterlife, but that means I bear the brunt of her madness."

"You can't leave the mansion?"

"I could, but I'd be abandoning the others to endure a nightmare. I won't do that to them."

"Kathleen doesn't deserve you." Tatyana zipped up her suitcase. "I wish I could do something to help."

"Do you know any exorcists?" Nick meant it to be humorous, but it came out more like a serious question.

"I wish." Tatyana picked up the suitcase. "I'm leaving now. It seems weird to say this, but it was a pleasure meeting you."

"Same here. I miss talking to someone other than Emelia and Kathleen. Will you be coming back?"

"Probably. Someday."

"I look forward to it." Nick walked over to the closed door, turned around, and waved to Tatyana. "Hopefully, I'll see you soon."

Nick backed up, disappearing into the wood.

✕   ✕   ✕

THE RIDE BACK to Dartmouth College was another pleasant drive through the Vermont countryside. Tatyana fell asleep half an hour into the trip and napped the rest of the way home. Julie dropped her off with little fanfare, wanting to get back to her place as quickly as possible.

Once back in her apartment, Tatyana quickly forgot about the events at Eden Hollow. She may have gone on a three-day weekend, but none of her stress did. Sorting through her mail, she found a collection notice from the electric company warning she had missed the last three bills and her service would be disconnected if they did not receive payment in full by Friday.

Turning on the cell phone she had left in her apartment, she had two voicemail messages. One was left by the secretary of graduate studies late Friday afternoon letting her know that the dean had scheduled a meeting for her in his office at ten o'clock Tuesday morning. The second was from her academic advisor on Saturday morning informing her about the Tuesday meeting. It didn't take long for that bastard Lasota to throw her under the bus. Why couldn't they have been from telemarketers pushing auto repair warranties?

Screw it. There was nothing she could do about it tonight. Tatyana unpacked, prepared an early dinner, and watched TV until she fell asleep.

CHAPTER ELEVEN

I DON'T CARE *who you are or how old you are*, thought Tatyana. *It's always unnerving when you get called to the principal's office. Or, in this case, the dean's office.*

She sat in the waiting room, wearing her only full-length dress, and matching heels, waiting for her appointment. The secretary typed away on her computer by the door to the inner office. Tatyana sat in one of three upholstered chairs positioned against the wall opposite the secretary so she could easily glance up and keep an eye on any visitors. Replicas of Thomas Kinkaid's *A Peaceful Retreat* and Monet's *The Artist's Garden at Giverny* hung on the walls beside and behind the secretary's desk.

Tatyana looked around for something to distract her attention, without luck. There were no magazines to thumb through. Attempting to chat with the secretary would be futile since she displayed the proper amount of professional courtesy mixed with polite disinterest. Tatyana glanced at her watch. Ten o'clock exactly. She hoped the dean's reputation for strict punctuality was true.

As if on cue, the desk phone rang. The secretary picked it up and listened.

"Yes, she's right here. I'll send her in." As the woman replaced the receiver, she smiled at Tatyana. "The dean will see you now."

Tatyana stood, straightened her dress, and entered the inner office.

Graham Philips, the dean of graduate studies at Dartmouth, stood and came around his desk to greet her. A man of average height and looks, he was impeccably dressed in a dark blue Hugo Boss suit, expensive silk tie, and Italian leather shoes. Philips had been a professor at the college who worked his way up into this position. A lot of the students and professors gossiped that he let his position go to his head. In reality, the dean's primary interest was the welfare of his graduate students. He wore the expensive attire to impress donors.

"Miss Reynolds, it's good to see you again." Philips extended his hand. "Thank you for coming."

"My pleasure." Tatyana shook it.

Dr. Heather Libby, her academic advisor, who sat in one of the chairs in front of the dean's desk, also stood and greeted Tatyana. With the introductions over, everyone took a seat.

Philips began the conversation. "We wanted to talk with you about your upcoming options since the internship with Dr. Lasota didn't pan out."

"What did he say?" she asked.

"Unfortunately, he's not able to accommodate you."

"Dr. Lasota was impressed with you," added Heather.

"He was?"

"Very much so. He said your academic record was exceptional and, with your personality, you would excel at an internship."

"Dr. Lasota called me right after your meeting on Friday," continued Philips. "He apologized for wasting your time. He really wanted to take you on but, according to him, he does not have the time this semester and is afraid you wouldn't get the best experience. However, Dr. Lasota said he might be willing to reconsider next semester."

"I see." Tatyana tampered down her anger. By singing her praises, the bastard had deflected any suspicions away from himself. If she complained about what had happened, then it would shine badly on her.

Both academics must have misinterpreted her fury as disappointment. Philips grew conciliatory. "I understand how upset you are. It's too late now to find you another internship. Dr. Libby and I have decided to move you to the top of the list for next semester."

"And this shouldn't hurt your academic career," chimed in Heather. "The original plan had been to do your internship this semester and then finish your doctorate. We can reverse the order. That way you can still graduate on time."

"Is that acceptable to you?" asked Philips.

It wasn't, but Tatyana couldn't admit that. Academically it was fine. She had already paid her tuition and would still graduate on time. Financially, though, this would kill her. She needed the internship, and not just to fulfill her requirements for her doctoral program. What she never told Julie or anyone else was that she had less than a hundred dollars in her bank account, which would not pay her overdue rent and utilities or buy her groceries. Without the funds that came with the internship, she would need to find another way to make money.

And quickly.

However, Tatyana couldn't relay any of this to the others in the room because it wasn't their concern and would make her look petty. Instead, she mustered the most positive attitude she could under the circumstances.

"That's fine with me."

Heather smiled.

Philips clapped his hands together. "Thank you."

"Thank you both for arranging this for me."

"It's our pleasure. You and Dr. Libby work out the details and I'll sign off on whatever you agree to." Philips stood and offered his hand again. "Let me know if there's anything I can do for you."

"I will."

Tatyana shook hands, made her way out of the office, said goodbye to the secretary, and walked back out onto Main

Street. To say she was seething would be an understatement. She wanted to storm back to Lasota's office and kick him so hard in the nuts that even his proctologist would never find them. It would make her feel better... a lot better... but would do nothing to advance her career. Instead, she opted to go back to her apartment, after first picking up a cheap bottle of wine and some pasta, then consider her options. Maybe tomorrow things would look brighter.

THINGS DID NOT look brighter in the morning. The sauce Tatyana had in her refrigerator had gone bad, so she had to eat her pasta doused in butter. Drinking the entire bottle of wine felt great at the time but, when she woke up with a hangover Wednesday morning, she regretted her decision. A cold shower, leftover buttery pasta, and two Tylenol later, she sat down in front of her laptop and went to back to working on her dissertation.

When Tatyana reached the point where she couldn't concentrate any longer and closed her computer, five hours had passed. She decided to reward herself with a walk and a latte at Starbucks on Main Street. She knew she didn't really have the money to spare but figured what the Hell, what difference would a few dollars make? Besides, it would help lessen the pain of her next task – finding a job.

Tatyana lucked out and got her favorite seat, the one in the front corner window with a view of the Nugget Theater. She loved to people watch and this was the ideal spot. Powering up her laptop, she began searching for jobs in the area, having already come to terms with rejoining the workforce if she didn't want to find herself and her few belongings on the street. The more time she spent online, however, the more frustrated she became with the fact that all the good-paying jobs were in southern New Hampshire, like Amazon in Manchester and

FedEx or UPS in Londonderry. They were all well over an hour away, not withstanding the fact she had already sold her car to make ends meet. All the jobs in Hanover or accessible by public transportation were mostly retail or restaurants, the former paying crap and the latter forcing her to rely on tips which, knowing her clumsiness, would leave her with nothing. Oh, well. She could always become a cam girl.

Tatyana stopped the depressing job search and opened her email, hoping a Nigerian prince had bequeathed her three million dollars, when her cell phone rang. She glanced at the screen but did not recognize the number. Damn telemarketers. She was about to place the phone back on the table when she noticed the call came from Eden, Vermont. Clicking the green accept button, she placed the phone against her ear.

"Hello?"

"Is this Tatyana?" The voice on the other end sounded afraid.

"Yes. Is that you, Annette?"

"It is. I need your help. All Hell had broken loose here at Eden Hollow."

CHAPTER TWELVE

"**W**HAT DO YOU mean all Hell has broken loose?"

Annette took a deep breath to steady her voice. "It began Sunday a few hours after you and Julie left. Kathleen roamed the mansion all night making noises. Neither Miss DeFelice nor I could get any sleep. On Monday, she became violent, slamming doors and knocking items off shelves. Yesterday, she pulled the phone wires out of the wall. We've never seen her this active before, and it's getting worse."

"You need to get Emelia out of there."

"That's the problem. We tried to leave yesterday but Kathleen wouldn't let us go. Every time Miss DeFelice approaches one of the exits, Kathleen locks the door. She blocked the front hall with a coatrack. When we attempted to sneak out through the kitchen, she hurled pots and pans at us. I'm scared that if we try again…." Annette's voice trailed off.

"Are you there?"

"I'm here."

"Are you still in the house?"

"No. I'm calling from the driveway on my cell phone. Apparently I can come and go as I please, but Miss DeFelice is forbidden to leave."

Tatyana thought for a moment. "Have you called the police?"

"I'm afraid to. The police won't believe us. They'll try to take Miss DeFelice away. God knows what Kathleen will do then."

"What I don't understand is why you're calling me."

"I overheard from the kitchen some of your conversations about your psychic connection with spirits and your interactions with Nick."

The confrontation with Kathleen on Sunday night rushed back into Tatyana's memory. "Do you think I caused this?"

"Please believe me, I'm not blaming you for anything. But you're the only Necroscope I know and the only one who can help."

Annette's use of the word Necroscope caught Tatyana's attention. "You have an understanding of the supernatural?"

"A little. You don't live in a haunted mansion without doing some research. Will you help us? Please."

"Of course, I will." Tatyana agreed even though she had no clue how to cleanse a house of ghosts, especially demented ones. "My only problem is I don't have a way of getting to Vermont. I sold my car and don't have enough money for a rental."

"Don't worry about that. I called Julie before you and left a voice mail explaining the situation. I'm sure she'll drive you up. If not, I'll come get you."

"You can't leave Emelia alone. I'll arrange something and call you back the minute I have definite plans."

"Thank you so much." The tears in Annette's voice could be heard over the connection. "Please hurry. I'm terrified, both for myself and Miss DeFelice."

"I'll be there as soon as I can. I promise."

Tatyana ended the call and placed her phone back on the table. As she shut down her laptop, the phone rang again. This time it was Julie.

"Did you talk to Annette?" she asked frantically.

"I just got off the phone with her. She explained the situation to me."

"What's going on?" Julie practically yelled over the phone, so loud that the young man at the table opposite Tatyana glanced over.

Tatyana explained everything Annette had related, doing so in as calm a tone as possible so as not to upset her friend. It didn't work.

"I cancelled all my meetings for the rest of the week," Julie rambled. "It'll take me several hours to get to you."

"That's okay. Drive carefully. You're no good to your grandmother if you get into an accident."

That brought Julie back to reality. "I will. Thank you for agreeing to do this. Do you think you can help?"

"I'll do my best. I promise."

"I appreciate that. I'll call you when I'm about thirty minutes from your place." The connection went dead.

Tatyana slid her phone into her jacket pocket and the laptop back into its case, cleaned her table, and exited onto Main Street, heading back to the college. She meant it when she promised Julie she would do her best to help Emelia. The problem was, while she had the ability to talk with spirits, she did not have the faintest idea on how to cleanse them from someone's home, especially a spirit as malevolent as Kathleen.

Thankfully, she knew someone who might be able to help.

CHAPTER THIRTEEN

TATYANA MADE HER way across the college commons, her mind distracted as scores of questions raced through her thoughts. She should have written them down rather than trust them to memory. Unfortunately, there was no time. She had called Dr. Alicia Talbott, one of the professors in the History Department, to see if they could meet this afternoon. The only time Dr. Talbott had available was lunch. Tatyana raced to get there in time.

Dr. Talbott was an anomaly on campus, a professor well respected yet viewed as an eccentric. Loved and admired by colleagues and students alike, she had been lecturing at Dartmouth for close to forty years. Having been asked on several occasions to be the head of the department, she politely declined each invitation, saying teaching was her only love. Over the years, she had taught various women-oriented courses, including the struggle for suffrage in the United States and how the various cultures of Islam treated women through-out the world. Her most popular course was the History of Witchcraft which, to some student's disappointment, was not a how-to class. Rumor had it that in her younger days she had performed spiritual cleansings and had even been good friends with Ed and Lorraine Warren. However, when questioned on the subject, she always smiled and said such activities were not viewed favorably in polite society.

Tatyana hoped Dr. Talbott would be able to help.

She arrived a few minutes early and stood outside the office, organizing her thoughts.

"Is that you, Tatyana?"

"Yes."

"Come on in."

Dr. Talbott's office was impeccably neat, unlike so many other professors. On one wall hung photographs of her at various locations in Salem and Europe associated with witchcraft. Two dreamcatchers hung from the ceiling, one by the door and the other by the window, which was partially open despite the chilled air. Unlike other history professors who kept historical artifacts on their shelves, she had a collection of crystals and amulets.

Dr. Talbott sat at her desk, a red sweater draped over her shoulders. For a moment, Alissa thought her efforts might be in vain. The woman did not appear to be a ghost hunter. Dignified and elegant, she wore an expensive pants suit and black heels. A pair of Christian Dior glasses hung from a strap around her neck. She had well-coiffured grey hair that hung down to her shoulders, the only indication of her age. She possessed a demeanor both positive and in control.

"Dr. Talbott, thank you for seeing me on such short notice."

"Please, call me Alicia." The woman pushed aside her lunch, a plastic bag full of baby carrots and celery, and shifted in her seat to give her guest her undivided attention. "May I call you Tatyana?"

"Yes. Thank you."

Alicia pointed to an empty seat by her desk. "What can I do for you?"

Tatyana spent the next ten minutes explaining the situation at Eden Hollow, her own encounters with the ghosts there, the current situation, and how she had agreed to help Emelia. Alicia said nothing during that time, taking in all the information. She waited until Tatyana had finished before asking questions.

"You felt these spirits in the house?"

"I saw them."

"How did they appear to you?"

"In flesh and blood."

"You mean they appeared to you in corporeal form?"

"Yes. When I first met Nick, I thought he was human."

"Interesting." Alicia pondered that statement for a few seconds. "Is this the first time you've had contact with the spirit world?"

"No. I've been to friends' houses where I felt spirits reaching out to me, and once at Gettysburg the ghosts of dead soldiers tried to contact me. It was especially prominent at Devil's Den."

"You have a special gift." Alicia studied Tatyana. "Is Eden Hollow the first time the spirits appeared to you?"

"Yes."

Alicia nodded. "How can I be of assistance?"

Damn, thought Tatyana. *This is where I get let down nicely.* "I heard you used to participate in spiritual cleansings. I was hoping you could give me some advice."

"I performed such rituals for close to thirty years but gave it up. It's a young person's game. As for giving you advice, in your situation you'll need much more than what I can pass on in an hour."

"Are you saying I need an exorcist?"

Alicia chuckled. "No. That's for demons and requires years of training by the Catholic Church. What are your religious beliefs?"

"I was raised Roman Catholic."

"That's not what I asked. Do you attend church or believe in God?"

Tatyana flushed with embarrassment. "I haven't been to church since high school."

"And God?"

"I haven't really thought about it."

"I'll take that as a no." Alicia frowned. "Are you spiritual in

55

any way? Buddhism? Paganism?"

Tatyana shook her head.

"What you're attempting is next to impossible. You're dealing with a highly malevolent spirit who has it in for you. Plus, you're an amateur. No offense intended. I have a deep belief in the spirit world and am a pagan myself. I studied this subject for years before attempting my first cleansing. You'll need to call on a deity or an extremely positive force more powerful than this spirit if you hope to win."

"Are you saying I could make matters worse?"

"It's possible."

Tatyana felt her hopes crashing down around her. "Is there anything you can do to help me?"

"Unfortunately, this isn't something you can learn from a do-it-yourself, fifteen-minute YouTube video. I teach a private course on spiritual cleansing and it takes months to prepare my students."

"Please. I'm desperate."

Alicia studied Tatyana. "You're going to do this whether or not I help you, right?"

"I can't leave Emelia like this."

A grin pierced the doctor's lips. "I give you credit. You have courage and determination. I hope it's enough."

Alicia turned to her desk and jotted down a list of items that would be needed to perform a cleansing and handed it to Tatyana. "First thing, you need to pick these up. Without them, you have no chance of succeeding. Pour a circle of salt around the exterior of the house. That creates a boundary that the spirit, once removed, can't cross to return to the location. Given the power of the spirit you described to me, I'd also place crystals in all four corners of the property, the house, and, as an added measure, the room where the spirit is most prominent. Tell the crystals that they must cleanse the house of evil."

"Seriously?"

"Yes. It's vital that you're confident in yourself and your abilities, which will be hard with no previous experience. We all have the ability to control the space around us. I don't know if anyone else in the house is spiritual but, if they are, have them join you. You want to create a positive hold space around you that negative energy can't penetrate. Once you control that positive energy, you can tell the malevolent spirit to leave. If you fail, then the evil energy will gain control over the situation and you."

"Okay." Tatyana said it with more confidence than she felt.

"Holy relics are also important but. However, since you don't believe in religion, they will not be as effective. Use holy phrases to gain control. Since you were raised Catholic, I'd use *The Bible,* especially Psalms 51. Since Holy water may be ineffective because of your lack of faith, use olive oil. I described how to apply it on that paper I gave you. Another thing you can do is burn white sage around the house. It cleanses the space and brings back the feminine energy."

"Feminine energy?"

"Yes. It's not a male versus female issue. Feminine energy is more powerful and positive than masculine energy, which tends toward evil."

"That's a lot to take in."

"I told you this isn't for amateurs."

"Anything else?"

"You need to gain control of the situation from the beginning. You must assume the roll of matriarch and not let the spirit get the upper hand. Do you know the malevolent spirit's name?"

"It's Kathleen,"

"Use it often. It'll allow you to gain control over the spirit. You always need to dominate it." Alicia leaned back in her seat. "Unfortunately, that's all I have for you right now."

"Thank you so much." Tatyana fought back the urge to hug the professor. "You don't know how much this means to me."

"I hope you succeed. One more thing."

Alicia opened her desk drawer and removed a white jewelry box that she handed to Tatyana. Tatyana opened it. Inside sat an amulet made of bronze in the shape of a pentagram set within a circle. A white crystal was imbedded in the center of the pentagram.

"What's this?"

"It's the amulet I wore when I did spiritual cleansings."

"Isn't the pentagram the sign of the devil?"

"Not necessarily. It's also a symbol of faith for Wiccans, which I adhere to. The crystal is Selenite. It's a strong crystal that emits a vibration which generates positive energy and helps ward off evil spirits. Unlike other crystals, it doesn't need to be recharged after every use. Keep it on you all the time. It's your best defense against a malevolent spirit."

Tatyana placed the cover back on the box and slid it into her coat pocket. "Thank you so much. You have no idea how much I appreciate this."

"You're welcome. And best of luck. You'll need it."

Tatyana left and headed back to her apartment. She had a lot to do before Julie showed up.

CHAPTER FOURTEEN

TATYANA AND JULIE did not set out for Eden until early next morning, partly because Julie didn't arrive at her apartment until a little after midnight, and partly because Tatyana needed to pick up specific items to conduct a house cleansing. It took several hours and visits to three different stores to purchase everything required, which meant they did not arrive at Eden Hollow until early afternoon.

Tatyana called Annette when they reached the outskirts of town to let her know they'd be arriving soon. As Julie parked the Mercedes in front of the mansion, Annette came out to meet them.

"I'm so glad you finally made it," she huffed, racing up to the car.

Tatyana opened the trunk and removed her suitcase and a travel bag filled with spiritual supplies. "Sorry, we're late. We had to pick up certain things for the ritual."

"As long as you're here. Things got scary last night." Annette glanced over her shoulder at the mansion. "I don't know if it's because Kathleen is angry that I called you or things are getting progressively worse."

"Fill me in."

"The first three nights, Kathleen made her presence known throughout the house, making noises, slamming doors, turning off lights. Last night…." A pained expression crossed Annette's face. "Last night she went after Miss DeFelice."

"Is grandma okay?" asked Julie.

"Physically, yes. But she's extremely upset by what's going

on."

"How did she go after Emelia?" asked Tatyana.

Annette closed her eyes as if trying to forget the image in her mind. "She invaded Miss DeFelice's bedroom, concentrating all her disturbances on that one area. Finally, around one in the morning, I brought Miss DeFelice down to the sitting room and stayed with her for the rest of the evening. Kathleen still roamed around the rest of the mansion creating a fuss but left us alone."

"How are things now?"

"Quiet. They always seem to be quiet during the day. It's at night that the horror begins."

Tatyana checked her watch. "It's about five hours until sundown."

"Will that give you enough time to set up?" asked Julie.

"More than enough."

Annette led the way inside the mansion.

The moment Tatyana stepped through the doorway she sensed the disturbances. The auras of the other spirits were more pronounced than during her first visit. This time they were not benign, a gentle hum in the background. The house reeked of spectral terror and it all focused on Kathleen, the fear over what she might do, and the uncertainty of their fates. She tried to detect Nick's aura but could not. Mentally, Tatyana called out to him, but got no response. She feared he had either left the mansion or that Kathleen had done something—

An icy cold blast of air washed over Tatyana. She recognized the seething hatred as that of Kathleen, the same detestation she had experienced on Saturday night, only greatly intensified. The malevolence wrapped itself around Tatyana and tried to push her toward the door, forcing her out of the mansion. Being incorporeal, it had no effect. Kathleen tried even harder but could not budge the woman. Tatyana mentally pushed back, which only angered Kathleen further. The hatred grew darker and more intense, threatening to engulf Tatyana's soul. She closed her eyes and concentrated.

"Get away from me!" barked Tatyana.

The spirit retreated, disappearing into the mansion but not leaving. Tatyana felt it lurking in the background.

"Are you okay?" asked Julie.

Tatyana opened her eyes. Julie and Annette stared at her, concern in their expressions. Both women had stepped back after her outburst.

"I'm fine. Kathleen was trying to push me out of the house. I pushed back."

"Is she gone?"

Tatyana shook her head. "It's going to take a lot more than yelling at the bitch to get rid of her. We still—"

"What are you doing here?"

All eyes turned toward the entrance to the sitting room. Emelia shuffled out, the courtesy she had shown over the weekend long vanished.

"I invited them back." Annette crossed the hall to her.

Emelia shooed Annette away with her right hand and circled around her, confronting Tatyana. "Haven't you caused enough trouble already?"

"Grandma, she came back to help."

"Help? She's the cause of all this."

"How did I cause this?" Tatyana asked in a calm, understanding tone.

"By talking with Nick on Friday night."

"I honestly had no idea." Tatyana looked at Julie and Annette, then back to Emelia. "Nick dropped by my room to say hello. I didn't know our talk would result in all this."

Emelia moved closer. At first, Tatyana was concerned the older woman might slap her. Instead, Emelia offered a wane smile and tenderly squeezed her hand.

"Please forgive me for lashing out at you."

Emelia turned back to the sitting room and motioned for the two women to follow. As they did, Annette picked up their bags and moved them upstairs to the rooms they had stayed in over the weekend. Emelia pointed to the wing-backed chairs in front of the roaring fire. The food cart sat beside Emelia's chair, carrying the dirty plates from her lunch which Annette had not yet removed.

Tatyana studied the older woman. The strain of the past few days showed. Dark circles had formed under Emelia's eyes and the lids were puffy from lack of sleep. Her gait was unsteady. Even her demeanor seemed strange as if she had aged years in a matter of days.

"Again, I apologize for my outburst." Emelia struggled to sit down. "I've gotten very little sleep since you left."

"I'm sorry." Tatyana leaned forward and rested her elbows on her knees. "I truly am."

"It isn't your fault. If I'm mad at anybody, it should be Nick. He started all this by talking to you in the first place. He knows how cra... what Kathleen is like."

A low rumble echoed through the walls.

"What is she like, grandma?"

"Extremely jealous."

"I don't understand," said Julie. "I thought Kathleen had the affair, not Nick."

"She did. Nick came back from overseas and walked in on them. He beat up her lover and Kathleen went with him to the hospital. When she returned, Nick was going to leave her. That's why she killed him, to keep him from going."

"Why is she so jealous if she cheated on him?"

"It has nothing to do with the affair," said Tatyana. "It's about the inheritance."

Emelia looked confused. "Nick never said anything about that."

"He mentioned it my last night here. His grandfather had passed away and left him two hundred thousand dollars. When Nick told Kathleen that he planned on divorcing her because of the affair and she would never see any of the money, she murdered him."

Julie nodded. "So, if Kathleen couldn't have Nick and his money, no one could."

"Exactly."

"It's been that way since I've lived here," said Emelia. "No one, not even the other spirits, can talk to Nick. Annette has never spoken with him."

"But don't you talk to him all the time?"

Emelia turned to her granddaughter. "Nick struck a bargain with Kathleen. If Kathleen left everyone in the house alone, he would never abandon her. I'm exempt because I'm too old to be a threat. It worked perfectly until he appeared in Tatyana's room this past weekend. That sent Kathleen into a fit of jealousy that she's taking out on us."

Tatyana rested her head in her hands. "This doesn't make any sense."

"There is no common sense when you're dealing with someone who's...." Emelia twirled her forefinger in circles by her temple.

Another low rumble shook the mansion.

"Grandma, why didn't you call us earlier?"

"I didn't want either of you girls coming back, especially you, Tatyana."

"Why me?"

"Kathleen is furious with you. I was afraid she'd attempt to hurt you. Annette made the call without my knowledge."

"I'm glad she did, Grandma. Tatyana will be able to put an end to this."

A sense of hope blossomed in Emelia. "Do you think so?"

"Yes." Tatyana spoke the words with far more confidence than she felt.

Emelia clasped her hands together. "Thank you. Thank you so much."

"It's my pleasure."

"It'll be your death." The voice that spoke was deep and

guttural, the words dripping with loathing.

The three women searched the sitting room for their source. Julie glanced over at the mirror above the fireplace and gasped. Tatyana spun around, taken aback by the image that greeted her.

Kathleen's face formed inside the mirror. The image was transparent, more like the outline of a human face than an actual reflection. It reminded her of the prop mirrors she had seen in carnival haunted houses, only this one was colored red, its features changing expression, and its eyes boring in on Tatyana. Even as a ghostly apparition, she could make out the hatred, anger, and jealousy in Kathleen's features. Even more disturbing, she felt its malevolence burning into her soul.

Emelia and Julie jumped out of their seats and backed away into the middle of the room. Tatyana stood and approached the mirror. "I'm not scared of you."

"You should be."

"Like I'm afraid of a cheap whore who cheats on her husband."

Kathleen grit her teeth and growled. Tatyana sensed her icy breath emanating from the mirror. "I'm going to enjoy this."

"Killing me?"

"That's a means to an end. Once your dead, your soul will be trapped in this house forever, allowing me to torment you for eternity." A sadistic laugh followed the taunt.

Tatyana fought back her terror and focused on what Alicia had told her. The only way to deal with evil spirits was to confront and challenge them. Summoning her courage, she backed away from the mirror until she reached the food cart. Her hands felt around until she found what she needed.

"Kathleen, you are not welcome here."

Another sadistic laugh. "You cannot ban me from this house so easily."

"I'm not trying to." Tatyana unscrewed the top of the salt

container and emptied the contents into her left hand. "I want you to leave us alone and go back to wherever you reside in this house."

"The entire house belongs to me."

Tatyana stepped toward the mirror. "I order you to leave us alone."

Kathleen grinned maliciously. "Make me."

Moving her left hand from behind her back, Tatyana tossed a handful of salt against the mirror. "Go!"

The crystals struck the surface. Kathleen growled and retreated, disappearing into the depths of the mirror. When she did, the frame shook violently, detaching from its wall mount. The mirror dropped onto the mantle, teetered for a moment, and fell forward. Tatyana jumped back a second before it crashed to the floor, shattering into hundreds of pieces.

Tatyana turned to face Emelia. "Are you okay?"

"Just a little shaken, thank you."

Julie stared at the broken mirror. "Did Kathleen just try to...?"

"Kill me?"

Julie nodded.

"I think so."

"How do you kids say it?" asked Emelia. "Things just got real."

"I'm afraid so." Tatyana focused on Julie. "I need to go upstairs and prepare for tonight."

CHAPTER FIFTEEN

TATYANA SAT ON the edge of her bed in the guest room, wondering how she had gotten herself into such a mess.

That's an easy one to answer, she thought. *You always take on more than you can handle.*

She had always been that way, like when she worked two part time jobs while an undergraduate student, or the summer she took four courses to graduate on time. Overextending herself was her worst personality flaw. None of it had been easy, and to get through she had sacrificed such luxuries as sleep and a social life. Only this time, it could get her killed.

She studied the items laid out across her bed. Thirty containers of kosher salt. Four dozen sage candles. A box of Selenite crystals. A package of white sage and an abalone shell to burn it in. A bottle of olive oil and a ceramic bowl. And the amulet Alicia had given her. Everything Alicia had told her she needed to cleanse Kathleen from the mansion.

Easier said than done. This would be like giving her an automatic weapon, dropping her in the middle of a SEAL Team, and telling her she would be going on a covert operation. She knew the rudimentaries of how they worked but had none of the technical expertise or experience to use them properly. Such a scenario would get her killed in a combat situation. Not to quibble about details, but in a few hours she would be heading into a combat situation with all the weapons she needed and no clue how to use them properly. Kathleen was going to kick her ass.

"You have to stop thinking that way."

The voice came from the doorway. Nick leaned against the frame. He smiled when they made eye contact.

"Stop thinking what way?" Tatyana asked.

"You can't second guess yourself if you want to banish Kathleen. She has become evil incarnate over the years. Her spirit is dark, way darker than the night she killed me." Nick motioned to the bed. "You're not going to get rid of her with salt and candles. You're in way over your head. Stop deceiving yourself."

"I have to do something to help Emelia. I caused this."

"No, you didn't. I did by talking to you. I'm the only one who can put an end to this."

"That's what Emelia said."

"That's what I told her because it's true. Can I come in?"

"Sure." Tatyana tapped a spot on the mattress beside her.

"Considering what's going on, I'll sit over here." Nick sat in the wing-backed chair. "Kathleen is angry with me because I talked to you. It'll take a while, but I can return things back to normal."

"How long is a while?"

"Three, maybe four months."

"And you expect me to let Emelia be tormented for several months until your wife calms down? You know I can't allow that."

"It might take less time. I just have to reassure her I'm still in love with her."

"Except you're not."

Nick cast her a stern glance. "That's not true."

"Now who's deceiving themselves?"

Nick's gaze fell to the floor.

"And even if Kathleen did stop bothering Emelia, what about you—"

"I'll be fine."

"—and the other spirits? You'll all be stuck here, terrorized by her."

Nick pushed himself out of the chair, turned to look out the window, and sighed. "You don't understand what you're dealing with. This isn't a situation where some old person died in their sleep and stayed behind because they don't know where to go. Everyone who passed away in this house did so in an extremely violent manner. This house has a vibe about it that's... that's...."

"Evil?"

"Unnatural. This place is filled with angst, sorrow, and depression. Kathleen feeds off that. It's what gives her the strength she needs to dominate us."

"I've read the newspaper articles about the deaths."

Nick turned from the window. "They're watered down. You have no idea how much anguish exists in this mansion. How much negative energy feeds Kathleen. How powerful it makes her."

"Can you show me?"

Nick paused. "I can let you experience the horrors that took place here. Are you sure you're up to it?"

"I need to know what I'm dealing with if I'm going to fight her."

Nick moved closer. "I need to enter your body to do this. Is that okay?"

Tatyana inhaled deep and held her breath. "How does that work?"

"I bind my soul with yours for a few minutes. I'll be able to show you what happened to each of the spirits consigned here."

"Will you be able to see into my soul, read my thoughts?"

"I could, but I promise not to."

After a moment of reflection, Tatyana nodded. "Let's do it."

Nick stepped close to Tatyana as if he were about to kiss her. "This could be scary for you. If you want me to stop tell me and I'll unbind our souls."

Tatyana took a deep breath. "Okay."

Nick merged into Tatyana. As the apparition visually disappeared, she felt him enter her mind. Tatyana closed her eyes. For a moment, she saw flashes of combat from World War II. Naval vessels engaged in evasive maneuvers. Flak blackened the sky as a massive dog fight took place overhead. The only thing she could hear was the staccato roar of thousands of weapons firing at the enemy. A fighter with large red circles on its wings broke free from the other aircraft and dove on the vessel. As it drew closer, she waited for it to release a bomb, which it never did. The men in the gun mount one deck below aimed their quadruple-barrel weapon toward the aircraft, peppering it with antiaircraft fire. Fear overcame her, accompanied by a desperate prayer that the gunners would destroy their target. The aircraft's right wing broke away and the fuselage burst into flames, yet the pilot still aimed his aircraft at the vessel. She heard the roar of its engines and the air racing across its remaining wing despite the gunfire all around. For a split second, Tatyana saw the pilot inside his cockpit, smiling. Anger replaced fear, a deep, bitter hatred for the enemy. The men in the gun mount screamed and tried to run, but it was too late. The aircraft crashed directly on the weapon. Three of the men were crushed by the fuselage and two were ripped apart by the explosion, body parts being flung across the deck and bulkhead in a splatter of blood. She ducked behind the gunwale a second before a fireball washed over her. The smell of burning aviation fuel and charred bodies filled her nostrils, making her nauseous. Then everything went blank.

Another image entered her mind. Tatyana walked through the mansion. She recognized the third-floor hallway. Passing a mirror, she glanced over at the image. An elderly woman stared back at her, the face haggard, circles under her eyes. She wore her white hair in a meticulously manicured bun and sported a Victorian-era dress, old but still in pristine condition. Several emotions washed over her at once. Depression, loneliness, and determination.

At the end of the hall, the woman opened a door to a stairwell leading to the roof. At the top of the stairs, she pushed open a hatch in the ceiling. Sunlight poured into the stairwell, accompanied by a pleasant breeze. A moment later, she stood on the widow's walk atop the mansion, stopping at the center. The town, much smaller and comprised of old buildings, spread out before her. The depression and loneliness faded away, being replaced with an unsettling contentment.

"We'll be together soon, my beloved."

The woman climbed over the railing of the widow's walk. Tatyana mentally screamed not to do it but had no control over the woman's actions. The woman's body leaned forward and dropped from the widow's walk. Excruciating pain wracked her body as it hit the roof, breaking several of her fragile bones. The body slid down the tiles then plummeted three stories before crashing onto the stone steps below. This time the pain became unbearable as more bones shattered and internal organs ruptured. The agony lasted several seconds before a feeling of peace filled her soul, then the image went blank.

Tatyana found herself in a basement room, the wallpaper gaudily designed, with nothing in it except a bed and a nightstand with a lamp. She sat on the bed. Before her stood a man wearing a 1920s style suit that reminded her of the old gangster movies she had watched as a child. He could be called anything but attractive, with a pockmarked face, a three-inch scar on his left cheek, greasy slicked-back hair, and a paunch that strained against his shirt and suit vest. His demeanor seemed even more unpleasant, exuding arrogance, hate, violence. He stared into the mirror as he knotted his necktie, a lit cigarette dangling between his lips.

Tatyana saw the reflection of the woman who sat on the bed. She was beautiful, or, more appropriately, had been at one time. The silky black hair cut into a bob now had a scraggily quality to it. The dark circles under the eyes and the slightly hollow cheeks attested to how rough times had taken their toll on her good looks. She wore nothing but black heels, nylons, and a red laced garter belt.

"I hope you had a good time," she said.

The man shrugged. "It was alright, Cheryl."

Cheryl squashed the anger and self-contempt that welled up inside her. "That'll be ten dollars."

The man reached into his pocket, removed a five-dollar bill, and placed it on the nightstand. "Here."

Cheryl picked it up. "Wait a minute. You still owe me five."

"That's all you're getting."

"My fee is ten dollars."

"That's all you worth. Shut up before I take that from you."

"Screw you. I'm telling Brian."

Cheryl stood and headed for the door, pulling a red silk robe from off the bed. A hand grabbed her and spun her around. Before she could respond, the man slapped her across the face. A welt formed on her cheek and one of her teeth became loose. He shook her violently.

"Don't talk back to me, you filthy whore."

He slapped her again, this time across the other cheek, and harder. His eyes seethed with anger. Cheryl was terrified.

"Let me go."

The man tossed her on the bed and stepped closer, towering over her. He loosened his necktie.

"Get out of here!"

This time the man punched Cheryl in the face. She felt her nose shatter and lost vison in her left eye. Blood trickled down the back of her throat.

Crawling on top of her, the man undid his necktie and wrapped it three times around her neck, then yanked the ends. The fabric tightened, cutting off her air supply. Panic overwhelmed her. She clutched at the tie with her left hand, trying to loosen its grip. With her right, she reached up and ran her long fingernails across his cheek, tearing open four claw marks in the skin.

"Son of a bitch! You'll pay for that, whore."

The man punched her three more times in the face. The first blow knocked loose two teeth that slid down her throat, gagging her. The second broke her lip in four places. The third rendered her semi-unconscious.

A voice came from the doorway. "Jesus, Tony. What are you doin'?"

"Shut up." The man grabbed the two ends of the necktie and resumed strangling Cheryl, only now she was too battered to fight. The man in the doorway stepped back into the hall but still watched. Cheryl reached out to him, her eyes begging for help. He did nothing.

Cheryl choked and gasped for air, unable to breathe through her restricted airway. She wedged her fingers between her neck and the tie, trying to rip it away, but had no energy left. Her vision narrowed and went black. She felt nothing.

The image faded out and retuned, this time inside a room. Tatyana recognized it as her guest bedroom by the configuration of the windows and the location of the radiator. Flames engulfed the inner walls and door. Thick black smoke filled the top third of the room, churning in violent eddies, threatening to suffocate her. Tatyana felt small, uncertain, and terrified. Her heart pounded inside her chest and she struggled to breath through the smoke and intense heat. She sat in the corner, a woman's arms around her, presumably her mother. A man made his way to the door and grabbed the knob, screaming in pain and clutching his hand. She saw the enflamed skin and welts forming on his palm and fingers. He rushed over to the bed and removed the blanket.

"Lay on the floor," he yelled. "There's more air down there."

The woman pushed her onto the floor. She breathed easier but it did nothing to quell the fear inside her.

"Antonio, are you in there?" The voice came from outside their room.

"Mr. Dobbs, is that you?"

"I came to help. Stand back."

The door opened. Dobbs stood in the doorway, a blanket draped over his body to protect him from the flames. Before he could move, the remaining air inside the room fueled the conflagration. The flames covering the walls exploded, dousing Dobbs and his blanket. He cried out and tossed the covering aside. His clothes were afire. Running into the room, he collapsed on the floor, rolling around to put out the flames. Antonio rushed forward and patted down the flames with his own blanket, eventually extinguishing the fire. It was too late. Dobbs lay there dead, his body smoldering, blisters forming on his face and hands. The stench of burnt flesh seeped into her nose.

Antonio spun around. "Maria, open the window. We'll have to jump."

"We're on the third floor."

"It's our only—"

The creaking of wood preceded the collapse of half the ceiling, burying Antonio. He didn't move.

The girl cried out and tried to crawl to her father. Maria held her back.

"He's dead, Gabriella. We have to get out of here."

Maria pulled her off the floor, ran to the window, and opened it. The sudden burst of pure air ignited the fire again. The flames exploded, blowing out the glass and covering Gabriella and her mother. The nightgown seared off Gabriella's body in seconds. The skin, muscles, and tissues burned more slowly as the intense heat evaporated the water within her. Once her body had dried out, the epidermis caught fire, burning off and peeling away. The blood in her veins and arteries dried out and clotted, clogging her circulatory system. A few seconds later, those same veins and arteries began to melt. Next, the dermis ignited, shrinking under the heat and bursting open, the fissures leaking fat. She inhaled. The heated air dried out her mouth and lungs, depriving her of oxygen. She gasped for breath, unable to take in air, thrashing about in panic. Finally, after several seconds of agony, she slumped forward onto the floor, fire consuming her tiny body.

She closed her eyes and screamed.

When Tatyana opened them, she saw Nick standing in the center of the bedroom with his back to her.

"Nick," the woman whispered.

He refused to look at her. "What do you want?"

"I want to talk."

"There's nothing to talk about."

"I want to explain what happened."

"Are you going to try to explain how you've been fucking another guy for over three years and went with him to the hospital rather than stay with me?" Nick raised the cigarette to his lips, dropping the tube of spent ash onto the carpet. He took a long drag and blew smoke onto the curtains. "You made your choice and I made mine."

"What do you mean?"

"I'm going back to Navy. I'll start a new life for myself and you can be happy with Joel."

"I don't want to lose you."

"You should have thought about that three years ago."

"What about your inheritance from your grandfather?"

"You'll never see a dime of that."

"I'll fight you for it in court."

He laughed derisively. "Good luck. Not many judges will look favorably on a cheating whore."

Kathleen gasped, partly from anger and partly from the realization she had forfeited a fortune. A moment later, she sniffed back a tear. "I'm sorry."

"Too late for that now."

"I know something that will make it right."

"What?" Nick spun around to confront her. His eyes widened in horror.

Kathleen struck him on the side of the head with the steel poker she had taken from the fireplace in the sitting room. She heard his skull crack. Blood flowed from his temple, staining his naval uniform. She struck Nick three more times with the poker until he stared at her with lifeless eyes before dropping to the floor. She hovered over him, focusing on his corpse. She felt nothing but hatred and intense, raging jealousy.

"If I can't have you and your money, no one will."

Her own soul had gone cold with the lack of humanity.

"What's going on in… oh my God."

Kathleen spun around. Two men stood in the doorway, frozen with fear by the sight that greeted them. Raising the poker above her head, she lunged at the closest of the two men and drove the tip into his right shoulder. The man screamed and dropped to the floor. She felt a terrible sense of glee.

The second man moved to stop her. Kathleen swung the poker like a baseball bat. He raised his arm in defense. The metal handle fractured his arm. He retreated into the hallway. She followed, hatred filling her soul, determined to kill the intruder.

Once in the hall, a third man moved in from the side and grabbed the poker. She thrashed about, trying to break his grip, but he was too strong. The man yanked the poker out of her hand, brandished it so the handle faced her, and smashed her in the face. She felt her forehead crack. Frantic with malice, she lunged at the man. He didn't expect such a move and was knocked onto his back. She fell on top of him, knocking the air from his lungs. He released the poker. Grabbing it, she raised it over her head, ready to kill.

Three gunshots rang out farther down the hall. Each bullet found their mark, punching into Kathleen's chest. She felt her stomach rupture and her lungs collapse. Glancing up, a fourth man stood ten feet away, a Colt .45 aimed at her.

"Drop the poker," he ordered.

Kathleen did not have the strength to continue the fight. She knew she had only moments left to live. She let go of the poker, which fell to the floor with a heavy clank. Spinning around, she ran back into the room, collapsing from exhaustion after a few feet. She ignored the man she had wounded. She pulled herself across the floor to Nick, clasping his dead hand in hers.

"Now we'll be together for eternity and no one else will have you."

The last ounce of life drained from her body.

Nick exited Tatyana's body. Tatyana felt a sense of relieve, although the nightmare was far from over. She no longer experienced the fear, anguish, and physical torment of the others who had died in this house, although the emotions stayed with her, deeply imprinted on her soul. Stumbling over to the bed, she dropped onto the edge, afraid she might pass out from what she had endured. Her head spun from dizziness. She closed her eyes to steady herself. Only then did she realize how fast her heart pounded. Inhaling deeply, she held her breath for ten seconds and slowly exhaled. The stress technique did little to lessen her anxiety.

"Are you okay?" asked Nick.

"Give me a minute, please." Slowly her heart rate returned to normal and the confusing thoughts and emotions settled down. When she opened her eyes, Nick stood in front of her, concerned.

"How are you feeling?"

"I had no idea how much violence had taken place in this house."

"I warned you. This place is cursed."

"It's not cursed," answered Tatyana, remembering what Alicia had told her about the accumulation of negative energy. "I have to cleanse the mansion of its bad aura."

"Good luck with that."

"What do you mean?"

"Kathleen thrives on that aura. She rules over everyone here, living and dead. She channels all the suffering and fear that has taken place here to make herself powerful. I can barely restrain her. Now that you're here, she's enraged."

"You don't think I'm up to this, do you?"

Nick's expression changed, the uncertainty in his eyes belying his words. "I hope you are. You've seen what she's capable of. She's become even more unstable in death, and more powerful."

Tatyana said nothing. There was nothing she could say.

Nick made his way to the door, pausing a moment before leaving. "I'm here for you if you need me."

He stepped through into the hall, his form morphing into a mist that dissipated.

Tatyana turned to the items laid out on the mattress, wondering what type of nightmare she had gotten herself into.

CHAPTER SIXTEEN

TATYANA DID NOT sleep at all that night for obvious reasons. She didn't even get undressed. Instead, she sat up in bed all night with every light in the room on, surrounded by her spirit cleansing materials. She had never been so happy to see the first rays of dawn flow through her window. When she heard mumbled voices and the clattering of dishes from the first floor, Tatyana packed the salt and crystals in her travel bag and headed down for breakfast.

Julie and Emelia were already seated at the table and Annette had served tea.

"Morning," said Julie, raising a steaming cup to greet her friend. "We thought you had overslept."

"No chance of that. I didn't sleep much last night." Tatyana stepped over to the table, placed the travel bag on the floor, and took a seat.

"Me neither. I was afraid to doze off."

"There was definitely a bad vibe around here last night." Emelia dropped a sugar cube in her tea and stirred it. "It kept me up for a few hours. And I didn't sense Nick around last night."

"Nick was with me." Tatyana chuckled. That would have sounded dirty if she had not been referring to a ghost. "He showed me what happened to the spirits trapped here."

"He never told me any details, but he said it was horrible."

"There's a lot of misery connected to this house."

"Is that why you're leaving?" Emelia's gaze fell to the travel bag.

"I'm not leaving. After breakfast, I'm going outside to prepare for tonight's cleansing. Those are the things I need."

"You have no idea how much I appreciate you doing this
for me."

"It's our pleasure."

Julie raised an eyebrow. "Our?"

"I could use your help outside."

"It's cold."

Emelia huffed. "Bring a jacket with you."

"Okay. I give up." Julie raised her hands in mock surrender. "As long as you don't use me as a sacrifice."

"That'll be later tonight," joked Tatyana.

Annette came out with breakfast – pancakes with maple
syrup and butter, cinnamon oatmeal, and slices of melon.
Tatyana could get used to eating this well all the time.

"Emelia," she asked. "Have you ever met any of the other
spirits?"

The elderly woman shook her head. "Just Nick. He won't
let Kathleen talk to me. It's part of their arrangement. The
others avoid me out of fear of angering her. I wouldn't even
know they existed if Nick hadn't told me. Every now and then I
feel a wave of negativity wash over me for no reason. I always
assume it's Kathleen's presence, though she has never made
herself known to me."

"You're lucky."

"Why do you ask, dear?"

"I was curious, that's all."

"Enough ghost talk." Emelia pointed to Tatyana's plate.
"Enjoy your meal."

× × ×

AFTER BREAKFAST, TATYANA and Julie chatted with their host
for a while. When Emelia excused herself, the two women
grabbed the travel bag and headed outside. They walked down

to where the circular driveway connected with the access road leading into Eden. Tatyana opened the travel bag, removed a container of kosher salt, and opened the spout.

"Do you know how many acres your grandmother owns?"

"Twenty, maybe thirty. I'm not sure."

"Any idea where the property line is?"

Julie shrugged.

Tatyana handed her friend the travel bag. "Follow me."

Starting at the left side of the driveway, Tatyana slowly circled the property, pouring the salt in a thin line. When one container was empty, Julie switched it out with a new one. After nearly an hour, the two women came back to where they had started. Tatyana poured the last section of salt across the asphalt, connecting it with the starting point. She handed the partially empty container to Julie, stepped back from the circle, and raised her arms beside her like a pastor calling his flock to order.

"Your job is to protect this property, and Emelia and Annette, from all spirits, benign and malevolent. Once the house is cleansed, you are not to allow any spirits back onto the property. I know you'll do as I ask."

Tatyana lowered her arms.

"I think this place has finally gotten to you," said Julie. "You're nuts."

"Ha ha." She turned to her friend. "You're supposed to tell the crystals what you want them to do."

"Why? Will they run away if you don't?"

Tatyana cast her friend a disapproving look. "Sometimes crystals have multiple uses so you have to tune them in to what they are required to do."

"And they understand you?"

"No. I create an aura of what needs to be done by talking and the crystals respond to that."

"You learned all this from your professor?"

"And from some research I did on the Internet before you

picked me up."

"Ghost Hunting for Dummies," Julie joked. "Now I really feel confident."

Tatyana reached into the bag and removed the box filled with Selenite crystals. She selected the four largest and slipped them into her pocket.

"What are those?" asked Julie.

"Selenite crystals. They're powerful at warding off spirits. You place them in the corners of the property, the residence, and the room where the spirit spends most of its time. Once they're driven away, these crystals prevent them from retuning."

"I thought that's what the salt was for."

"It is. You use these when dealing with more powerful spirits."

"Like Kathleen."

"Exactly." Tatyana placed the box back in the travel bag. "Go on inside. I'll join you in a few minutes."

Tatyana walked to the corner of the property to the left of the front facade, staying close to the tree line. Removing one of the crystals, she placed it on the grass, stepped back, and raised her arms.

"Your job is to be the watchtower for this property. Assist the salt circle in protecting the residence, and Emelia and Annette, from all spirits, benign and malevolent. Once the house is cleansed, you are not to allow any spirits back onto the property. I know you'll do as I ask."

Tatyana repeated the same ritual in the other three corners of the property. Once back inside the house, she performed the same ritual on the first floor in the four corners of the house, using the medium-sized crystals, as well as in the four corners of her room where Kathleen was most prevalent. Julie followed behind her, handing her friend what she needed.

With the crystals in place, Tatyana headed for the front door. Julie waited on the front porch. She removed a bottle of olive oil and a small ceramic bowl, poured some of the olive oil into the latter, and placed the bottle back into the travel bag. Dipping her finger in the bowl, she ran a line along the floor in front of the door and repeated the process along the door frame, then did the same to the exterior.

"Once the spirits are expelled from this house, your job is to block any spirits from entering. Protect the residence, and Emelia and Annette, from all spirits, benign and malevolent. You are not to allow any spirits back onto the property. I know you'll do as I ask."

Tatyana performed the same ritual to all the entrances to the house, including the door leading to the widow's walk. She completed the same task on the interior frames to all the windows and both sides of the doors to each room.

When finished, Tatyana collapsed on her mattress. "I'm exhausted. What time is it?"

Julie placed the travel bag on the floor by the bed and checked her watch. "It's a quarter to one."

"It seems later."

"That's because you got no sleep last night."

"I'm going to take a nap. I'll need my energy for tonight."

"We both will," said Julie.

"What do you mean?"

"You're doing this for my grandmother. What type of friend would I be if I didn't help you? What time are we performing this exorcism?"

Tatyana did not bother to correct her friend. "Once your grandmother goes to bed."

"Perfect. Then I'm going to take a nap as well. I'll swing by and wake you for supper. See you in a few hours."

Tatyana laid her back on the pillow, trying not to let self-doubt overwhelm her. She rationalized that being nervous was only natural since this would be her first spiritual cleansing. Mentally she compared this experience to her first time driving a car. The thought of getting behind the steering wheel terrified her but, once on the road, she took to it naturally. The same would be true tonight. All she needed was to have confidence in herself. She could handle this.

Fortunately for Tatyana, she was more tired than nervous, and fell asleep after a few minutes.

CHAPTER SEVENTEEN

D INNER THAT NIGHT was tense. Everybody knew what would happen in the next few hours but no one wanted to discuss it. The conversation was strained, focusing on benign topics to distract them. Tatyana could not even remember what they had for dinner. It was delicious, but she barely touched the meal, her mind focused elsewhere.

Emelia and Annette went to bed early, the only acknowledgement of what was about to take place being both women wishing their visitors good luck. With them gone, Tatyana went through the house and opened every window, accept the ones in Emelia's room, to make it easier for the spirits to escape. In each room, she lit a sage candle and placed it in a holder. Half an hour later, Tatyana and Julie stood in the guest bedroom building up the courage to begin the cleansing.

Tatyana removed an abalone shell from the travel bag, crushed white sage into it, and set it on fire. She waited several minutes for the whisps of white smoke to fill the room then handed the shell to Julie.

"Are you ready?" asked Tatyana.

"No. What do you want me to do?"

"Nothing. Just hold the shell and be here for moral support."

"That I can handle."

Tatyana stepped into the middle of the guest bedroom.

"Kathleen Thompson, you are not welcome in this household. I demand you leave this residence and never return."

Silence.

"Do you think it worked?" asked Julie.

"I wish." Tatyana turned and faced the door into the hall. "Kathleen Thompson. I banish you from this house and command you never to return."

Silence.

"Kathleen Thompson, do you hear me?"

"I hear you. I don't deem you worthy of a response." The voice, foreboding and condescending, came from the corner near the bathroom.

"I have control over you."

"You have control over *nothing*."

A mist appeared in the corner near the ceiling, growing and shaping itself until it formed a ghostly image of Kathleen. It slowly descended and crossed the room, landing on the floor at the foot of the bed. Julie jumped up and moved beside Tatyana. The apparition moved around the bed, morphing into the corporeal form of Kathleen, much like Nick had done at their first meeting. She had a malicious smile on her, the glare in her eyes malevolent. She approached the two women, stopping three feet from them. Julie stepped back.

Tatyana held her ground. "You are not welcome here."

"Maybe not, but I'm staying."

"No/ you're not. I command you to leave this house."

Kathleen laughed, a sound so evil it made Tatyana's blood run cold.

"You have no control over me."

"I do. You're merely an entity. It's time for you to move on."

"I'm the essence of this house. I decide who stays and who goes. You're the intruder. If you're smart, you'll leave while you have the chance."

"I banish you from here."

"Didn't you learn anything from your mentor, little one?" Kathleen circled Tatyana, like a shark approaching its prey. "You need spiritual power to have any sway over me. A lapsed

Catholic and a college whore is no match for me."

Tatyana was dumbstruck. "What do you mean?"

"I know all about you, little one. My soul is joined with the soul of every entity in this house. When Nick melded with you, he gave me access to your thoughts. He may not have delved into your mind, but I did."

"She's trying to rattle you," warned Julie.

"Am I?" Kathleen stepped in front of Tatyana. Her face inches from the young woman. "You resented your mother because she raised you as a strict Roman Catholic. She forced you to go the Mass everyday and refused to let you date. You never resolved your conflict with her before she died and have been tormented by that regret ever since. Of course, that didn't stop you from being a slut your first three years in college. How many men did you sleep with? Fifteen? Twenty? I couldn't count them all in the short time I was in your mind. But you were a wild one. You did things that would have appalled your mother and offended your so-called God."

"Shut up."

"Do you think she knows about that three-way you had with your boyfriend and his buddy at the frat party?"

"I said, shut up."

"Or the abortion you had in your junior year?"

"Shut up!"

Kathleen laughed again. "He was a winner. What was his name? Bradley? No, Brady. When you told him about being pregnant, he blew you off and said you had slept with so many guys it probably wasn't his. You had quite a reputation, didn't you?"

"Damn you." Tatyana lunged at Kathleen, ready to slap her. Instead, she passed through the spirit, finding herself by the bed. In that moment, she sensed the darkness that filled Kathleen's soul. Hatred. Fury. Revenge. And self-loathing. She had grossly underestimated the evil of the spirit she now faced.

"I don't know whether I should laugh at you or feel pity for you."

Tatyana closed her eyes and ignored the taunts, trying to clear her mind. She needed to regain the upper hand.

"Stop listening to the bitch," said Julie.

Kathleen spun around to face Julie. She strode toward the women, forcing her back toward the window. Her voice seethed with anger.

"You're of no consequence to me. If you insist on interfering, I have no qualms about tormenting you, but I'll take no pleasure in it."

"Get away from me." Julie fell into the wing-backed chair by the window and dropped the shell on the floor. Kathleen towered over her.

Kathleen leaned forward and stretched out her hand, holding it in front of the woman's face. "Maybe I should meld with your soul and discover your dark secrets."

Julie pressed herself into the chair. "Tatyana!"

Tatyana had removed the open salt container from the travel bag and poured some into her hand. She turned from the bed.

"Your argument is with me."

"You're right." Kathleen wagged a finger in front of Julie's face before turning to face Tatyana. "I'm going to teach you not to—"

Tatyana threw salt into Kathleen's face. "You are no longer welcome here."

The entity screamed, though Tatyana could not tell whether from pain or anger. The room became intensely cold. Julie wrapped her arms around her chest.

Tatyana approached Kathleen and pointed to the window. "Be gone from here!"

Her corporeal image dissipated. A moment later, the room temperature returned to normal.

Julie cautiously stood. "Is she gone?"

"I hope so. At least she's not a threat to us any—"

A scream came from the second floor.

"Grandma."

Both women raced downstairs and burst into Emelia's room without knocking. The room had become icy cold. Emelia sat in her chair, terrified. The book she had been reading lay face down on the rug, some of its pages folded over. As they watched, the book elevated and flew toward the chair. It would have hit Emelia in the face if she had not blocked it with her hands. Julie rushed over to protect her grandmother.

Annette entered. "What's going on? I heard a scream."

The door slammed shut, trapping them inside.

Kathleen's spectral image appeared in the mirror, her face contorted in fury.

"I'm not the one who is going to leave. You are."

Tatyana grabbed the lamp from the end table by the chair and flung it at the mirror. The glass shattered.

"You are not welcome in this home."

An angry cry echoed through the room. The mirror frame rattled and fell off the wall, barely missing Julie and Emelia. Shards of broken mirror spread across the floor.

Every loose item in the room – the cosmetics on the bureau, the lamp Tatyana had thrown, the sundries on the nightstand, the discarded book, the mirror frame – elevated. A vortex formed in the corner near the ceiling. The sundry items began spinning around the room above Emelia.

Annette rushed over to help. One of the lamps shot out of the whirlwind and struck her in the temple. Blood poured from a gash in her forehead.

"Get Emelia out of here," yelled Tatyana.

Julie lifted her grandmother from the chair and both women rushed to the door. Annette spun around and grabbed the knob. The door would not budge.

Kathleen's voice filled the room. "I'm not the one leaving."

The mirror frame shot from the whirlwind, aimed at Tatyana. She turned at the last second and shifted her body.

The frame slammed into her back. A jolt of pain shot down her back and left arm. Thankfully, nothing was broken.

"Do something," yelled Julie. Tatyana had never seen her friend so scared.

Another lamp hurtled toward Emelia. Annette pushed it out of the way at the last second.

"We'll leave," conceded Tatyana.

The bedroom door opened.

Annette and Julie ushered Emelia out into the hall and down the stairs. Tatyana rushed after her, praying Kathleen would allow her to go. A handheld mirror flew across the room, catching her in the back of the head as she exited. The glass shattered but none of the shards became imbedded in her scalp.

The others had already opened the front door and made their way down the steps toward Julie's Mercedes. Just as Tatyana reached the entrance, the door closed on her. She tried the knob but it would not open.

"Do not taunt me, little one. If you ever return here, *you will die.*"

The door opened and Tatyana raced out.

Annette helped Emelia into the back seat of the car and joined her. Julie sat in the driver's seat. She started the engine and waved for her friend to join them. Tatyana did not need to be told twice. She jumped into the passenger's seat. Before she had closed the door, Julie shifted into gear and sped down the circular driveway.

Tatyana looked at the house one final time in the side mirror.

This was not over.

CHAPTER EIGHTEEN

THEY DROVE TO Stowe, the closest town with a motel. Julie rented a room with two king-sized beds. Once set up in their room, Tatyana agreed to stay and keep an eye on Emelia while Julie took Annette to the hospital to have the doctors treat her head wound. While Tatyana and Emelia waited for them to return, they sat on the beds watching television. Tatyana had found an old movie, *Yankee Doodle Dandy* with James Cagney. The musical seemed to help Emelia take her mind off their predicament.

Tatyana could not reconcile herself with the fact that she had failed so miserably and ruined Emelia's life. Not only had her visit to the house angered Kathleen, but her amateurish attempts to cleanse the house made it unlivable. Now they were all stuck at a Commodores Inn in Stowe. She had underestimated the maliciousness of Kathleen as much as she had overestimated her own abilities. If only she had listened to Alicia when the professor warned her she was in over her head.

"I don't blame you for any of this, dear."

Tatyana snapped out of her reverie. "I'm sorry?"

Emelia glanced over at her and smiled. "I don't blame you for this. Nick tried to warn me about Kathleen. I never believed him. Since I had never seen any bad intentions I assumed he exaggerated given how their relationship ended."

"Thank you, but none of this would have happened if I hadn't shown up."

"Anyone could have been the catalyst for her outrage. It could as easily have been Julie. Nick decided to talk with you.

Don't blame yourself."

"It's hard not to. I drove you from your home."

"Kathleen drove me from home. You only tried to help. I'm grateful that you did."

"I still need to make things right."

"I know you will if you can. As long as you don't put yourself in any danger."

An awkward silence fell over the room as Emelia went back to watching her musical. It was only broken half an hour later when Julie returned.

Tatyana jumped out of bed to greet her friend. "How's Annette?"

"She's fine." Julie slipped off her jacket and dropped it by the chair next to the door. "The wound required nine stitches but she'll be fine."

"Where is she?" asked Emelia.

"The doctors are keeping her overnight for observation in case she has a concussion."

"That's good. She'll get some rest." Emelia smiled and went back to watching her movie.

Tatyana hugged her friend, holding her close. "I'm sorry."

"There's nothing for you to be sorry about."

Tears ran Tatyana's face as she broke the embrace. "I screwed up everything."

"Kathleen did."

"That's what I told her," added Emelia.

"Grandma, do you mind if we talk in private?"

"Go ahead."

Julie opened the door and motioned for Tatyana to follow. They strolled down the corridor.

"I wanted to talk to you about what Kathleen said regarding your college years."

Tatyana broke down in tears. "I'm so embarrassed."

"Don't be. You have nothing to be embarrassed about."

"I made so many bad choices those three years."

"We've all done things we later regret."

"Even you?"

"Yes."

"Still, you must think so little of me."

"On the contrary. You're one of the strongest willed people I know." The two women entered the lobby and Julie pointed to a pair of seats in the corner where no one could hear them. As they sat, she continued. "What I wanted to say is you can't let Kathleen get under your skin. That woman is psychotic and a manipulator. She made you doubt yourself and, when that didn't work, she went after the people you care about. You showed more courage back there then I did."

"Courage? I ran."

"You gave up the fight to protect the rest of us. Knowing when to fall back takes more guts then staying in a losing battle."

Tatyana offered her a weak smile and squeezed Julie's hand. "Thanks."

"What are friends for?"

Tatyana paused, debating whether she wanted to ask the next question. "I need to ask a favor."

"Anything."

"I want to borrow your car."

"Sure. What for?"

Tatyana locked her gaze on Julie. "I'm going back to Eden Hollow and exorcise that bitch."

"I'll come with you."

"You need to stay here with Emelia and keep her safe. Besides, if you come along, Kathleen can use you against me. I stand a better chance if I go on my own."

Julie removed the keys from here pocket and handed them to her friend. "Are you sure?"

Tatyana nodded. "I have to do this."

"Are you going back tonight?"

"Too dangerous. Kathleen is most powerful at night. I'm

going back tomorrow afternoon to confront her. There are two things I have to do in the morning."

✕　✕　✕

AFTER A FITFUL night's sleep and a breakfast that consisted mostly of coffee, Tatyana completed the first of her two errands – driving to the nearest Walmart to get necessities for the rest of her group. That included two days' worth of food and water as well as clothes for Emelia and Annette so they could change out of their nightgowns. All of it purchased, of course, with Julie's credit card.

She brought the essentials back to the hotel and made certain Julie and Emelia were settled in. Julie would hire a taxi and pick up Annette at the hospital once the doctors released her. Once certain they were okay, Tatyana left for her second destination.

St. Theresa's Catholic Church in Eden Hills.

Tatyana parked out front and stared at the building. It was what one would expect of a Catholic church in a small parish, welcoming yet less grandeur than compared to the one she had attended as a child. That should be an advantage, this church being less intimidating. However, given that she wanted a clean slate to give her the greatest advantage possible, this seemed as daunting as her upcoming confrontation with Kathleen. Shutting off the ignition, she exited the Mercedes and entered St. Theresa's.

The interior was set up like any other Catholic church, only smaller. Tatyana entered the last row of pews, feeling too self-conscious to make her way down front. She knelt on the cushioned kneeler and crossed herself. Building up the courage for the nest step, she rose and crossed the nave to the confessionals along the left aisle, entering and closing the door behind her. She waited for the priest. Nearly a minute passed. A part of Tatyana was relieved. She prepared to leave when a figure emerged on the other side of the latticed opening.

"Thank you for being patient, my child. You may proceed."

"In the name of the Father, and the Son, and the Holy Spirit, Amen. Bless me Father for I have sinned. It's been nearly ten years since my last confession. I'm a graduate student at Dartmouth College working toward my Doctorate. During my first three years of college, I slept with many men and once had an abortion. Back then, I also smoked marijuana and drank heavily."

"Do you still commit such sins?"

"Not since my junior year in college, which was seven years ago."

"Ten years is a long time to not attend church. Why have you been away so long?"

Tatyana hesitated to answer.

"You can talk to me. I'm here to listen to your confessions and absolve you of your sins, not judge you."

"Father, I lost my faith years ago. My mother was strict when it came to her faith. I was not allowed to date in high school and had to attend Mass every day. Religion became a burden to me rather than a way of life. I stopped going to church when I went away to college."

"Which is when you rebelled and became intimate with so many men."

"Exactly."

"That's a natural reaction, my child. Do not let those sins weigh too heavily on your soul. Have you talked to your mother about this and cleared any resentment between you?"

"I can't, Father. She died years ago."

"I'm sorry to hear that. I'm sure she holds no animosity toward you in the afterlife."

Tatyana fought back her tears. "Thank you, Father."

"Are you seeking to return to the Church and reconnect with God?"

"I don't know, Father. I'm confused. At the moment, I need to cleanse my sins as much as possible."

"I can do that, my child. But your soul has no chance of salvation if you do not give yourself to Christ."

"I understand, Father."

"Do you remember your Hail Marys?"

"Yes."

"Then say ten Hail Marys and, as you do, open yourself to letting the Holy Spirit enter your soul."

"I will."

"Now pray your Act of Contrition."

Uncertain what to say, Tatyana recited from memory the Right of Penance she had memorized in school.

"My God, I am sorry for my sins with all my heart. In choosing to do wrong and failing to do good, I have sinned against you whom I should love above all things. I firmly intend, with your help, to do penance, to sin no more, and to avoid whatever leads me to sin. Our Savior Jesus Christ suffered and died for us. In his name, my God, have mercy."

"Then I absolve you of all your sins."

"Thank you, Father." Tatyana made the sign of the cross and closed with, "Amen."

As she stood to leave, the priest stopped her. "Before you go, are you in any danger?"

The question caught Tatyana by surprise. "What do you mean?"

"Your voice. I hear more fear in it than regret. And you said you need to cleanse your sins as much as possible. Is someone threatening you?"

She paused. "You'll laugh if I told you."

"I'd never laugh at a child of God, especially one who's in distress."

"I'm confronting an evil entity tonight."

"You're not exorcising a demon, are you?"

"No, Father. I'm cleansing a friend's house of a malevolent

spirit."

"What you're undertaking is extremely dangerous."

"I know. Can you offer any advice?"

The priest thought for a moment. He spoke in a low voice, almost conspiratorial. "As a representative of Christ on Earth, I'm compelled to tell you that your only chance of success is to trust in the power of the Lord. However, as a man who has witnessed exorcisms and spiritual cleansings while in seminary school, I can warn you that you have no chance of winning unless you embrace some positive form of energy, whether it's a deity, Mother Earth, crystals, whatever. Evil can only be conquered by good. The greater the evil, the greater the positive power that is needed to defeat it. I'll pray for you tonight. But you'll need to find a positive source to tap into if you hope to survive. I know you're not a believer, but I'll leave a bottle of Holy water by the exit. God be with you, my child."

Tatyana gave the priest a few minutes to perform his good deed. She exited the confessional and hurried out of the church back to the car, slipping the bottle of Holy water into her pants pocket on her way out. She spent the next two hours driving the back roads of northern Vermont, contemplating what the priest had told her and mentally working out a strategy for dealing with Kathleen.

TATYANA PULLED INTO the driveway leading to Eden Hollow an hour before sunset. Dark clouds moved in from the southwest, obscuring the sun. The lack of sunshine cast the tress in shadows, giving her the sensation of being watched as she drew closer. She forced herself to write off the thought as the figment of an overactive imagination.

Exiting through the tree line, she stopped before the circle of salt and stepped out of the Mercedes. The house loomed in front of her at the top of the hill, appearing more ominous then ever. The only sight that appeared somewhat comforting were the lights left on from last night that still shone through the windows. They served as a reminder of the horror that awaited her this evening.

Climbing back in the car, Tatyana headed up the circular driveway and parked in front in Eden Hollow.

CHAPTER NINETEEN

TATYANA STEPPED INSIDE the mansion. A cold sensation washed over her, accompanied by a steady hissing. She raised her sensory defenses to ward off an attack but stood down. No spirits were nearby. Tatyana realized that, in their haste to evacuate the house last night, they had left the windows open. The cold was a result of the chilled night air flowing through the screens. The hissing emanated from the radiators that worked furiously in a vain attempt to keep the house comfortable. She did not want to be around when Emelia received her next heating bill.

She checked out the sitting and dining rooms. The sage candles had burnt down or been blown out. She expected to find the same in the other rooms. Replacing them would be one of the many things she had to do before sundown.

Approaching the stairs, Tatyana climbed cautiously, taking one step at a time. Clearing her mind and opening her soul, she hoped to detect any spirits stalking her before they drew too close. Instead, she sensed nothing. Not even Nick's presence. Sure, it could have meant the cleansing last night had worked, that she and Julie had successfully driven away the ghosts, and that Kathleen's tantrum was a last show of defiance before her banishment. And some day she might meet a duke and marry into a European royal family. The more likely explanation? This was the calm before the paranormal storm, that Kathleen lay dormant until the battle began, and the other spirits were in hiding.

Tatyana reached the second-floor landing and paused.

Now she sensed the presence of Kathleen. The aura on this floor felt oppressive and the air hung thick, making it difficult to breathe. She felt a heaviness weigh against her chest and press on her head. Tatyana leaned forward and peered down the hall, half expecting Kathleen to lunge from the shadows. The house remained quiet and inactive.

Inching her way along the corridor, she stopped and tried the door to Emelia's bedroom. It opened. The room remained as they had left it last night, with all the items that had been swept up in the vortex laying on the floor where they were dropped. The lamp that had struck Annette in the head lay a few feet away, dried blood on the base. In the center of the room sat the mirror that had shattered against her back, the broken fragments reflecting the fading rays of sunlight. Tatyana felt the muscles in her shoulder stiffen, a reminder that she remained physically vulnerable to Kathleen's assaults and would need to be especially cautious tonight.

Moving up to the third floor, the oppressiveness became even greater. Tatyana made her way to the guest bedroom. The travel bag with her cleansing supplies lay on the bed. The abalone shell sat on the floor where Julie had dropped it when confronting Kathleen. The burning sage had singed the rug. Thank God it had not burned down the house.

She stepped inside. This room was much colder than the others because of the evil attached to it. She sensed a tinge of malevolence but not the presence of spirits, confirming this was the dark center of the haunting and would be Ground Zero for tonight's battle.

Picking up the shell and removing the bag from the mattress, Tatyana returned downstairs. She headed outside and checked the perimeter. The salt circle remained intact and the Selenite crystals lay where she had placed them. She repeated the commands for them to perform their required functions and went back inside.

This time, evil filled the rooms. The incantations must have intimidated Kathleen.

Tatyana went from room to room, burning white sage in the shell and strolling around so the mist filled all four corners. Before leaving, she replaced the sage candles and lit them, then repeat the commands for the indoor crystals and olive oil to keep out any spirits. An hour later, every room, closest, and open space in the house had been purified except the guest bedroom.

By now, an icy chill gripped the room. Tatyana anointed the doorways and window frames with more olive oil and spread extra salt across the door jamb and windowsills. She set up seven sage candles, one in each corner and one each on the dresser, nightstand, and the end table by the window. With that complete, she drew a circle of salt four feet in diameter in the open space between the bed and window. She stood inside the circle, placed the bag by her feet, and removed the abalone shell and white sage, which she lit. Tatyana waited until the mist had permeated the room before calling the final confrontation to begin.

"Kathleen, this is Tatyana. By all that is good and holy, I command you leave this house now and never return."

CHAPTER TWENTY

"**I** GIVE YOU credit, little one. You're persistent." Kathleen's voice echoed from deep within the residence, a low and threatening tone that rumbled through the walls. "Foolish, but persistent."

Tatyana slowly turned, searching for the location from which Kathleen would appear, keeping a wary eye on the corner of the room from which she had materialized last time. No images appeared. Maybe Kathleen feared her after all. Reaching into her back pocket, Tatyana removed a piece of paper and unfolded it. On it was a warfare prayer she had printed from the Internet for use in cleansing stubborn spirits. Tatyana took a deep breath to steady her nerves and began reciting.

"I address myself to the purest entities of the spiritual world. By all that is good and holy, I bow in humility before you and ask that you cover me with the white light and protection of the pure spirits. I claim the protection of this light for myself, for my friends, and for those who reside in this household. I take a stand against all that is evil and negative, especially the malevolent entity that shrouds this house in its darkness. In the name of the purest entities of the spiritual world, I command the vile entity inhabiting this residence to leave at once. I ban you from ever returning here."

A noise emanated from the second floor. It could have been a howl or the wind blowing through an open window. In either case, it sent a cold shiver down Tatyana's spine.

"I ask the purest entities of the spiritual world to grant me the power to overcome fear and darkness. Forgive my sins and imperfections, cleanse my soul, and imbue me with the courage to confront and defeat the vile entity before me. I seek complete and absolute victory over this evil and seek your help in banishing it from this residence as well as releasing the souls of the tormented spirits trapped here."

The howling reached the third floor and flowed down the hall. A cold chill blew into the room, the gust causing the candle flames to flicker.

"I give myself to the purest entities of the spiritual world. I refuse to show fear and back down from the darkness that haunts this house. I banish hate and anger from my own life. As shall it be with me, shall it be with this residence. I banish hate and anger from within these four walls and cast it back to the realms of darkness where it belongs."

Throughout the house, the electric lights shone brighter for a few seconds, as if being overcharged with energy. Tatyana sensed it in the air, like charged ions during a lightning storm. Except these ions surged with hatred, malice, and a desire for revenge. The lights surged bright one more time then blinked out, casting Eden Hollow in darkness. Only the seven sage candles in the room provided illumination.

A light shone in the hall, reflecting off the walls as it approached the bedroom. It wasn't generated from electricity or from candles. It had more of a natural glow to it, like a lightning bug, only much brighter, more intense, and less comforting. The light had a yellowish-red hue and increased in intensity as it approached.

"Purest entities of the spiritual world, grant me the strength and wisdom to banish this entity. Help me to thrust into Hell the vile spirit that dwells in this residence and thrives off the misery and suffering of those who are good and righteous."

Kathleen centered herself in the doorway, her gaze boring into Tatyana. She had not yet taken on corporeal form, remaining a shimmering image. The glow shifted from a yellowish red to intense white, which matched the anger and hatred that glared in the Kathleen's eyes.

"You came back, little one."

"You knew I would. I left only to get Emelia and the others to safety."

Kathleen entered the room and circled around Tatyana like a predator. "Do you really think a motel in Stowe is safe from me?"

The surprise must have been evident in Tatyana's expression.

"How did I know? You have so much to learn. I'm not confined to this location. Having bonded with Emelia, I can easily follow her anywhere she goes. If I wanted, I could be in that motel room haunting Emelia and Julie, or at the hospital with Annette. However, my issue is not with them. It's with you."

With the last three words, Kathleen stepped quickly toward the circle of salt. It took every ounce of will in Tatyana not to flinch.

"Kathleen, be gone from this house. You are not welcome here. You are evil and impure, a whore who ruined her own life and now wants to ruin the lives of others."

"I'm not a whore!" The entity surged toward the circle of salt, the human-like features fading, being replaced by blood-red eyes and a snarling mouth filled with pointed teeth.

"You belong in the darkest regions of the spiritual realm where you can do no harm to Emelia or anyone else. By the powers invested in me by the purest entities of the spiritual world, I command you to leave this residence at once and never return."

Kathleen laughed, an evil, guttural sound that terrified Tatyana. "You have no power over me. I'm much stronger than you. You're a pathetic soul, a child playing a game she doesn't fully understand."

Tatyana ignored the taunt and concentrated. "I call on the

purest entities of the spiritual world and command you to leave this residence at once and never return."

Kathleen stood at the outer edge of the circle of salt. "When I am done with you, when I've ripped your soul from your body and condemned it to reside in this damnable house for eternity, I'll go after Emelia and your friend Julie. I'll drive them to commit suicide, forever depriving them of solace, and will drag their spirits back here to be tormented forever. All because of *you*."

Tatyana knew that as long as she remained within the circle, she would be safe. She also knew she lacked the power and experience to banish Kathleen. She had lost control of the cleansing. Desperation and fear overwhelmed her. Closing her eyes, she cleared her mind of all negative thoughts and tried to find a resolution. She remembered what Alicia and the priest had told her – to defeat evil she needed to believe in a higher, more powerful entity. Obviously, she did not have enough faith in the spirit world. She recalled the one time she had faith as a child attending church. Back then she believed in God, his goodness and mercy, his power to forgive sins and combat evil. Tatyana went back to those days almost fifteen years ago and summoned the faith in the Lord she had as a child, a faith that she had flouted for so many years.

Tatyana opened her eyes and met Kathleen's malicious gaze. "In the name of God, the Father and the Almighty, his son Jesus who died for our sins and brought light into the world, and the Virgin Mary in whose purity she bore God's only son, I command you to leave this residence and never return."

Kathleen laughed. "An agnostic whore calling on God for help. How pathetic. Let's see if your God can help you now."

The entity stepped to the center of the room and focused on the sage candle on the end table. The flame turned red and grew to a height of two feet. Kathleen flicked out her fingers. The flame bent backward, touching the silk curtains. The material caught fire.

Tatyana rushed out of the circle of salt. Yanking the curtains off their rod, she dropped them on the floor and stomped on them until the flames were extinguished. Only then did she realize her vulnerability. She ran back to the safety of the circle, but Kathleen had inserted herself between the woman and her sanctuary. Tatyana stopped, uncertain what to do.

"Now, little one, you're going to experience the full fury of my wrath."

The bureau began to shake. A ghostly vortex appeared over the piece of furniture, like the one that had formed last night in Emelia's room. One by one, the drawers pulled free and became caught up in the whirlwind. Then they drawers shattered. Pointed shards of wood and chunks with rusty nails protruding circled menacingly.

"Where is your almighty God now?"

Tatyana braced herself as the pieces of the drawers hurtled toward her.

At the last second, the projectiles flew to the sides, passing Tatyana and slamming harmlessly into the other furniture and walls.

A familiar voice beside her yelled, "Enough!"

Nick stood beside Tatyana in his spiritual form. "Stop this now, Kathleen. Leave these people alone. It's their house."

"It's *my* house."

"No, it's not. We're merely trapped here. I beg of you, if you ever had any true feelings for me, move on and let these people be."

"I killed for you in this house and died here for you. I'm staying."

"We're not going to allow that." Nick spoke without anger or fear, only determination.

Kathleen chuckled derisively. "You and this whore are going to stop me?"

"We all are." Gabriella appeared on the other side of

Tatyana.

One by one, the other spirits consigned to the house appeared around Tatyana. Gabriella's parents and Mr. Dobbs, their clothes burned by fire, their skin deformed by blisters. Cheryl, her neck bruised from strangulation. Mrs. Wells, her body shattered and crippled by the fall from the widow's walk.

Nick positioned himself between Kathleen and Tatyana. "You've tormented us for years and we've had enough. This is your one chance. Leave this residence willingly."

"How dare you defy me!"

The room suddenly grew oppressive as the temperature dropped and the air was sucked out. Tatyana could hardly breathe. The pressure in her head was excruciating. Fear whelmed up inside her. She had no idea how she would defeat an entity as evil as Kathleen.

Gabriella stepped up beside her. "Do you trust me?"

"I do."

Gabriella smiled and her spirit merged with Tatyana.

A sense of solace and hope immediately washed over Tatyana. Fear and uncertainty dissolved.

Gabriella's parents, Antonio and Maria, joined her, filling the woman with familial love. Mr. Dobbs merged next, adding to the mixture heroism, a willingness to risk one's own live to save those of his friends. Cheryl went next. Though sensing self-loathing and fear, Tatyana also detected an intense courage to stand up and confront evil. The widow Wells entered last. Tatyana felt a love so pure and intense that this woman chose to die rather than live without her husband. These people were more than tormented souls. Even in death, they contained within them the purity inherent in mankind, the love, courage, and self-sacrifice that distinguished good from evil. These people had come together to help Tatyana tap into the Great Spirit, the essence of all that is kind and loving within ourselves.

"You will all regret this," Kathleen shouted derisively.

"You had your chance." Nick stepped back, merging with

Tatyana.

A confidence she had never experienced before filled her soul.

Tatyana focused her gaze on Kathleen. The spirit's self-confidence had eroded and fear glimmered in her eyes.

"Purest entities of the spiritual world, grant me the strength and wisdom to banish this vile entity. Help me to thrust into Hell the evil spirit that dwells in this residence and thrives off the misery and suffering of those who are good and righteous."

"I will not leave."

Tatyana took two steps forward. Kathleen retreated toward the door.

"Kathleen Thompson, you are not welcome in this household. In the name of the Great Spirit, I demand that you leave this residence and never return."

"No!" Kathleen moved into hall. This time she winced as she passed through the doorway anointed with salt and olive oil.

Tatyana followed.

"In the name of the Great Spirit and the purest entities of the spiritual world, I banish you from this residence to the darkest corners of the realm to which you belong."

Kathleen dropped to her knees. Her entity began to lose it forms, dissolving into a mist. The evil spirit who had murdered her own husband and tormented the souls of so many others had been shorn of her arrogance, kneeling like a penitent child and pleading for mercy. "I don't want to go."

Tatyana slid her hand into her pants pocket and removed the bottle of Holy water. Removing the cork, she flicked the container in Kathleen's direction, sprinkling her with the contents. As she did, the voices of the seven spirits inside Tatyana called out in unison.

"We banish you from this residence to the darkest corners of the realm to which you belong."

Kathleen's form collapsed into a swirling mist that spun in

the center of the hall.

Tatyana walked up to it. "Be gone from this residence and never return."

The mist cloud rapidly expanded until nothing remained. With it went the feeling of oppressiveness that hung so heavily over the house. No evil or negativity existed in the house, only a sense of lightness.

Tatyana felt at ease, more so than she had in years. She had done it. No, they had done it. The spirits trapped in this house had shown her the way, had introduced her to the Great Spirit and helped cleanse the property of evil.

Tatyana turned around. Seven spirits gathered in the hall. They all smiled. They no longer appeared as they had in death but in life. Antonio and Maria held hands. She sensed among the spirits a plethora of positive feelings. Happiness. Relief. Hope. Gratitude.

"Thank you," said Gabriella.

"For what?"

"For freeing us. You acknowledged us and the suffering we endured here. By banishing Kathleen, you released our trapped souls. Before we left, we wanted to express our gratitude."

Gabriella went to hug Tatyana, realizing at the last moment she was unable to. Instead, she offered a polite curtsy and rejoined the others.

As Tatyana watched, their images faded.

"Nick, wait."

All seven spirits dissolved into separate mists that melded together, floated into the bedroom, and flowed out the open window.

"Goodbye." Tatyana waved after them. "And good luck."

The lights in the house flickered for a moment and came back on, bathing the room in its soft glow. Tatyana moved toward the salt, pausing before entering its circle. She no longer needed the protection since the house was cleansed. The only discomfort came from the cold night air pouring through the windows which she easily remedied by shutting them. A familiar pinging and hissing filled the room along with heat emanating from the radiators. Tatyana pulled the wing-backed chair over to the radiator nearest her bed and dropped into the cushions.

She had earned a few minutes rest.

CHAPTER TWENTY-ONE

FATIGUED FROM HER confrontation with Kathleen and her lack of sleep the previous evening, Tatyana decided to retire early. Before going to bed, she closed the rest of the windows in the house and called Julie to inform her of the success of the cleansing. Part of her feared going to sleep in case Kathleen returned, an unfounded fear quickly overcome by exhaustion. Tatyana slept soundly, woken from a peaceful sleep by the morning sun streaming across her face.

She spent the morning preparing Eden Hollow for Emelia's return. She started with her own room, gathering the pieces of the broken drawers and placing them on the bureau, then folding and adding the burnt curtains to the pile. Next came Emelia's bedroom. She cleaned up as much as possible, wiping Annette's blood off the lamp, sweeping up the shards of broken mirror, and returning everything to its place. Anything damaged, she left in the corner for Emelia to decide what to do with.

With the physical part of the task done, Tatyana decided to reinforce the spiritual cleansing to ensure none of the spirits attempted to return later. She went from room to room, removing the burned-down sage candles and candle holders as well as performing a final ritual with the abalone shell and white sage. Opting to leave the Selene crystals around the mansion, she checked each one, making sure they remained in the proper place and reciting the command for them to serve as barriers to ward off evil.

Tatyana had finished bolstering the salt circle and crystal

watchtowers around the exterior when a taxi pulled up the driveway and parked behind Julie's Mercedes. To her surprise, Emelia and Annette climbed out of the back seat, the latter helping her mistress to the front steps. The driver made his way to the trunk and removed the shopping bags filled with their clothes. Julie joined him from the front seat, paid the man, then took the bags and fell in beside her grandmother and Annette, walking with them toward the front stairs.

Tatyana joined them. "I was coming to get you in an hour."

Julie motioned toward her grandmother. "Emelia wouldn't wait. She wanted to get back into her house." A pause ensued before she mouthed the words, "Is it safe?"

Tatyana nodded.

They followed as Annette helped Emelia up the front steps. The older woman entered and straightened. She sniffed. "It smells wonderful in here."

"That's white sage. I used it to cleanse the rooms."

"The musty odor is gone." Emelia grinned. "We left the windows open when we left, didn't we?"

"I'm afraid so."

Emelia used her right hand to brush the thought away. "The place needed to be aired out."

Emelia made her way into the sitting room and sat in her favorite chair by the fireplace. She closed her eyes and relaxed. A minute later, she opened them.

"Kathleen is gone. I can feel it. Was she difficult to get rid of?"

"Very. You'll have to replace the bureau, curtains, and rugs in the guest bedroom."

"A small price to pay to finally be rid of that bitch. Sadly, the other spirits are gone as well."

"Without the evil keeping them here, they left. Hopefully, their souls will finally find peace."

"I hope so. I'm really going to miss Nick, though."

Tatyana agreed with that sentiment, wishing she had a chance to say goodbye.

Annette came from upstairs and moved beside Tatyana. "Thank you for cleaning up Emelia's room."

"You're welcome. I didn't want her to pick up the mess. I placed those items that were broken in one corner."

"You did that for me?" asked Emelia.

"Yes."

Emelia flashed her granddaughter an I-told-you-so look. Julie rolled her eyes. Tatyana had no idea what to make of the exchange.

"After the spirits left, I cleansed the rooms one final time with white sage. The Selenite crystals are still in place inside the house and around the property. I commanded them crystals to prevent any spirits from re-entering the property, so you should have no more problems with hauntings. If you do, call me."

Emelia took Tatyana's hands and squeezed. "Thank you, my dear."

Tatyana turned to Annette. "I'm leaving an abalone shell and some white sage in the bag in my bedroom. I recommend cleansing every room in the house once a day for the first week and then once a week for a month."

"You'll have to show me how to perform the ritual."

"I can do that. It's easy."

"Then it's settled," said Emelia. "You and Julie will stay for lunch. After we eat, you can show Annette how to ward off the spirits."

✕   ✕   ✕

LUNCH HAD BEEN small and simple but, after living out of a motel room for more than a day, delicious. Emelia even asked Annette to join them. The conversation was a bit strained as the women talked about anything except what had happened the previous evening. Emelia remained content knowing the house was cleansed. As Tatyana later showed Annette how to perform the cleansing, she gave the woman a brief version of what happened so Annette realized the importance of continuing the ritual and letting her know if any spirits returned.

On the ride back to Hanover, Julie had barely made it to the end of the driveway before she asked, "What happened last night?"

Tatyana chuckled. "Do you want the theatrical version or the one edited for television?"

"The director's cut."

Tatyana obliged, filling in her friend on the events leading up to and including the battle royale. Julie said nothing, only occasionally glancing over to make certain her friend was serious. Tatyana finished telling the story as they passed the border between Vermont and New Hampshire.

All Julie could say was, "Wow. I thought the part I had experienced was intense."

"That was the tip of the iceberg."

"Do me a favor?"

"Sure."

"Next time you go to a spirit cleansing…." Julie looked over at her friend and smiled. "…have someone else drive you."

"Deal, but I don't see me doing this again anytime soon."

"You never know," teased Julie. "You might miss the thrill of it. Ghost hunting could become addictive for you, like sex."

"Really?"

"Or coffee."

"That one I'll give you."

Twenty minutes later, Julie pulled the Mercedes into the parking lot of Tatyana's apartment building and shifted into park.

"I know you have a long drive ahead of you, so I won't keep you." Tatyana opened the passenger door. "Thanks for the ride."

"Before you go." Julie reached into the backseat, brought her purse up front, and opened it. Removing an envelope, she handed it to her friend. "Emelia asked me to give this to you once we got back to Hanover."

Tatyana closed the door and opened the envelope. A stack of $100 bills filled it. She pulled out the money. "What's this?"

"Your fee for cleansing Eden Hollow."

"I didn't ask for any money."

"Grandma knew you'd be stubborn about it, which is why she asked me to wait until I got you home before giving it to you."

Tatyana ran the bills between her fingers. "There has to be a couple of thousand in here."

"Five, to be exact."

"I can't take this." She tried to give back the envelope.

Julie leaned against the door and raised her hands. "I'm not getting involved. If you don't want it, you can return it yourself. I'm not getting my grandmother mad at me. But if you ask me, you more than earned it."

"I don't know."

"Take it." Julie pushed the envelope back to her and gestured toward the apartment. "You know you need the money."

"Please thank Emelia for me." Tatyana leaned over and hugged her friend. "We need to get together soon for coffee."

"Just coffee. No ghosts."

Tatyana got out of the car, pulled her suitcase and travel bag out of the backseat, and headed into her building. Opening her apartment door, she flicked the light switch but nothing happened. Damn it, the electricity had been turned off. A perfect ending to her day.

Removing her cellphone from her pocket, she opened the flashlight app and used it to make her way into the kitchen. Rummaging through the cabinet drawer, she found a flashlight in which the batteries had died, but no spare batteries to refill it. Finding a candle, she removed it, searched for a box of matches, and, finding one buried in the back of the drawer, used it to light the wick. When the soft glow from the candle lit the room, she turned off her cellphone to conserve power.

"I always found candlelight romantic," said a familiar voice from the opposite corner of the kitchen.

Tatyana cried out and jumped back, banging into the kitchen counter and almost dropping the candle. "Damn it, Nick. Don't do that."

"Sorry." Nick raised his hands in surrender. "At least I waited until you lit the candle."

"Maybe you could have warned me first." Tatyana's heart rate returned to normal. She smiled. "I'm glad to see you, though."

"Good. I was afraid I wouldn't be welcome."

"Never. I couldn't have defeated Kathleen without you and the others. Thank you."

"I got the idea from Ephesians 6:11."

Tatyana raised an eyebrow. "I didn't picture you as the religious type."

"The ship's chaplain used to repeat it before going into battle. 'Put on the whole armor of God, that ye may be able to stand against the wiles of the Devil.' It worked in this case."

"It did." An awkward silence followed. "I suppose this is goodbye?"

"About that." Nick lowered his head, embarrassed, like a teenager about to ask out his first date. "Would you mind if I hung around for a little while?"

"You want to haunt me?"

"No," Nick said quickly. "Nothing like that. It's just that, when we bonded, I felt a strong connection with you. Under different circumstances, I think we would have been good friends. And I'm not talking about residing here, being around twenty-four hours a day, watching you when you take a shower—"

"Excuse me?"

"Forget I said that. I'd only come by if you summon me. To talk."

Tatyana thought for a moment. "I'd like that."

"Good." Nick smiled. "I'll also be able to help you on future cleansings."

"I won't be doing that again."

"Trust me. You will. So, is it a deal?"

"Yes, it's a deal."

"Great." Nick stepped forward and offered his hand, then pulled it back. Old habits die hard, even within the spirit world. "Can I call you Tats?"

"Only if I can call you Casper."

"Tatyana it is."

"Now, if you don't mind, I'm going to sleep. I don't let men into my bedroom on the first date anymore."

"I understand. Give me a call sometime."

Nick waved goodbye. His spiritual form dissolved into a mist that hung for a moment where he had stood before evaporating.

Tatyana picked up her candle and headed to the bedroom, nearly tripping on the pile of clothes scattered across the floor. Tomorrow morning, she would deposit Emelia's money in the bank, pay the electric bill, get the power restored, then come back and straighten up the apartment. She didn't want Nick to know what a slob she was.

As she crawled into bed, thankful to be in her own room, she pondered what Nick had said about doing more cleansings in the future. Despite her protestations to the contrary, the thought of working with the spiritual world excited her. She loved history. The incident at Emelia's house allowed her to interact with and be immersed in it. Cleansing spirits was a lot more exciting than reading textbooks and correcting term papers.

Besides, it felt fulfilling to help others in need.

PREVIEW OF *THE GHOSTS OF SALEM VILLAGE*

"W E'RE GOING TO do it in a parking lot again?" Debbie crossed her arms and huffed as John, her boyfriend, pulled his ten-year-old Honda Civic into Forest River Park.

"It never bothered you before."

"What an ass." She shifted to look out the passenger window.

"Come on. I'm joking."

"Everything's a joke with you."

John placed a hand on her knee and squeezed. Debbie slapped it away and moved her legs closer to the door.

"I'm sorry. Really. I know I can be a dick sometimes."

"Sometimes? That's an understatement."

If the insult bothered John, he didn't show it, which pissed off Debbie even more. Her anger shot through the roof when John pulled into a parking space beside a black Ford Escape. Their friends Tom and Cindy sat inside. Cindy smiled and waved.

Debbie turned to John. "I told you I'm not into that type of shit."

"Relax. We're here for a party, not an orgy."

A knocking on the passenger window caught Debbie's attention. Cindy stood by the window, motioning for her to lower it. When she did, Cindy leaned inside and hugged her friend.

"It's so good to see you."

Tom came over carrying a case of Coors under his arm, high-fiving John as he climbed out of the sedan. "You ready?"

John tore open the top of the case, pulled out a can, popped the top, and raised it in a toast. "Let's get this party started."

Debbie stepped out into the parking lot and glanced around. Forest Hill Park sat on the shore of Salem Harbor. It was an open area exposed for hundreds of feet. Nearly a dozen houses lined two sides of the park. The playground in front of them and the hill behind them with a scant covering of trees offered little protection, allowing anyone who lived in those houses to see what was going on. Any cop coming out of West Avenue had a clear of view of everything. Being the only two vehicles in the parking lot would draw a lot of attention, something none of them wanted during a beer binge since the oldest of them, Cindy, had only turned nineteen last month.

"We're gonna get caught if we stay out here," she warned.

Cindy took her arm. "That's why we're not drinking out here."

"Then where are we drinking?"

"In there." Tom pointed in front of him as he headed down a cement walkway.

"There" referred to a copse of trees in front of them. A six-foot-high fence composed of wooden slats ran along the edge of the tree line. At the end of the walkway stood an entry gate. Above it hung a wooden sign that read:

PIONEER VILLAGE Salem in 1630

"What is this place?" asked Debbie. "I've never heard of it."

Cindy giggled. "No one has."

"It was built in 1930 to commemorate Salem's three hundredth anniversary," answered Tom. "It supposedly looks the way Salem did during its first years. The city never tore it down and now it's a tourist attraction."

"How do you know all this?" asked Debbie.

"My older brother worked here last summer. He told me about it. Even better than that...." Tom reached into his pocket and withdrew something. "He gave me the key to get in."

Tom passed the case of beer to John then slid the key into the padlock. With a quick twist, it popped open. He looked at the girls and winked. "We're in."

Tom ushered them inside, closing the gate behind him. A duck pond sat to their right. They walked for several yards, crossing over a tiny foot bridge and entering a clearing. A one-room wooden building sat on the opposite side.

"What's that?" asked Cindy.

"It's the gift shop," Tom answered. "If you take off your shirt, I'll think about getting you a new one."

"No, you pervert." She playfully nudged him in the chest with her elbow. "I mean, what's in front of the gift shop."

"Those are pillories. Back in those days, if you were found guilty of a crime, you'd be placed in them in the town square so everyone could see your shame."

"I want to try." Cindy ran over to it.

Tom joined her. He lifted the upper board. Cindy placed her head in the larger groove and her wrists in the two smaller ones on either side. Tom lowered the board so she was trapped.

"Someone take a picture."

John placed the case of beer on the ground and removed his cell phone. Lining up the shot, he snapped a photo. The flash blinded them temporarily.

Debbie punched him in the arm. "Are you crazy? Someone might see that and call the cops."

"Relax. You're too wound up."

Cindy tried to pull free but couldn't. "Get me out of here. It's uncomfortable."

"It's supposed to be." Tom walked over to her and paused. "What's in it for me if I get you out?"

"If you don't get me out of here, you're not getting any tonight."

"Fair enough." Tom moved around to the back. Instead of

lifting the upper board, he shoved his crotch against Cindy's ass and began dry humping her from behind.

"Stop that!"

Tom continued his foolishness. "Hey, get a video of this."

"No!"

John took out his cell phone again.

"That's it," said Debbie, heading for the walkway. "I'm waiting in the car."

John rushed after her and stopped her at the bridge. "Come on. We're just having fun."

Debbie turned her back on him and crossed her arms over her chest again. John tried to hug her from behind but she pushed him away.

"I'm sorry. I'll be good."

Debbie couldn't stay mad at him. She spun around and gave him a kiss. "Okay. But watch it. We could get into big trouble for being here."

John took her hand and led her back to the others. Tom had already released Cindy. She couldn't have been too angry considering he had her pressed against the pillory with his hand up her sweater. On seeing their friends, they broke the embrace and straightened their clothes. Tom picked up the beer.

"Follow me."

They crossed another foot bridge, eventually stopping in front a two-story wooden building. The sign out front listed it as the governor's mansion. A run-down fence made from tree branches tied together with rope surrounded the property. Directly across from it sat a garden, enclosed by the same old-style fence, the ground frozen due to the winter weather. Two modern benches stood by the gate. Tom placed the case on the end of one of the benches and removed three cans, handing one to each of the girls and keeping the last for himself. The girls sat down and began drinking. John finished off his Coors, pulled out a second, popped it open, and took a long gulp.

Debbie glanced around. "Is this where they burned the witches?"

"Sure is." John spun around. Beer spilled from the top of the can onto his hand. "Right on this very spot."

"Don't listen to him," said Tom. "The witches in Salem weren't burned. They were hung."

"Like me." John grabbed his crotch.

Tom ignored him. "They burned witches in Europe, not here. Those killed in Salem were hanged on a hill near the CVS."

"But not here?"

Tom shook his head. "This place was a forest back then."

"Look at you," teased Cindy stood and wrapped her arm around his shoulder. "Good looking and smart. I hit the jackpot."

"Yes, you did." He leaned into Cindy and kissed her.

An uneasiness suddenly settled over Debbie. Something about this place did not feel right. The cold cut seeped under her skin, and not all of it was due to the weather.

"I don't feel comfortable here." She met John's gaze.

"Have another beer. That'll warm you up."

"I don't want a beer," she snapped. "I want to go home."

Cindy reached over and clasped her friend's hand. "Are you okay?"

"No. I have a bad feeling about being here."

Cindy turned to Tom. "Maybe we should go."

He nodded in agreement. "John, let's find another place to drink."

"You're all a bunch of pussies." John finished his beer, tossed the can aside, and removed a third one.

"Come on. Maybe we can drive down to Nahant—"

"Warlock!" John stepped back and pointed a finger at his friend, then broke into a drunken laugh. "You're possessed."

"John," said Debbie. "Stop it."

"Witch!"

Tom had enough. He tapped Cindy on the shoulder. "We're out of here. Debbie, do want a ride?"

"Thank you."

John dismissed them with a wave of his hand. "You're a bunch of Purigrims."

"Puritans," corrected Tom. He grabbed the case of beer and walked away. They fell in behind him.

"Wait. Wait." John picked up a stick from the ground in the shape of a Y. As he stepped toward the governor's mansion, he reached into his pocket, removed a lighter, and placed the flame against the wood. After a few seconds, the top of the stick caught fire. He held it in in front of his chest. "What am I?"

Tom sighed. "I don't know."

"I'm a witch."

Debbie grimaced. "That's sick."

John laughed. He moved the stick in a circle and bounced it up and down, mimicking a scream as he did so, as if it were a person on fire.

Tom took Cindy by the hand. "Let's go."

"Hold on." Debbie stepped closer to the governor's mansion.

"Leave him. He's an asshole."

"I don't care about him." Debbie pointed to the building. "What's that?"

All of them turned to the structure. A brilliant light shone inside. At first, they feared it might a night watchman who had caught them in the act. Yet the light didn't appear as though it came from something with a bulb but rather a candle. Only Debbie had never seen a candle that generated this much illumination.

The light passed by one of the windows on the second floor, moving into the hall and descending the stairs. It dimmed for a moment then brightened again when it reached the first floor, growing more intense as it neared the exit. Rather than the door opening, the light passed through the wood, emerging as a fluorescent, hovering sphere that descended the twin steps leading to the ground.

Debbie took a few steps back. Every rational part of her brain told her to run, but curiosity had gotten the better of her. She needed to know what was inside the sphere.

It floated across the yard toward John and began to morph, developing what appeared to be arms and legs. As it drew closer, the shape became more defined and gradually took on the form of a young woman in her mid-twenties. She wore a dark-colored dress made of wool that hugged her form, but not in a sensual manner. A white apron tied around her waist draped down to her knees. A white bonnet hung around her neck, bunched up on her pulled back blonde hair. The image never took corporeal form, shimmering like a hologram. It stopped ten feet from John and examined him, shifting its head from one side to the other.

"G… guys." John could not divert his gaze from the image that hovered in front of him. "Please tell me this is part of a light show."

"Back up slowly," advised Debbie.

John ignored her. He reached out a hand and extended it toward the spectral image. It pulled back a few feet and paused, staring at him. John moved closer. This time she allowed him to touch her. His hand passed through. John jerked it back.

"What's wrong?" Debbie asked.

"It's cold. Like sticking your hand into iced water." John held his hand over the burning stick to warm it.

The spectral image focused its gaze on the stick. Its eyes widened, then shifted onto John. The cool, white glow darkened, taking on a harsh, yellowish hue. Its eyes glared red and locked onto him. The pretty face of the young woman shifted into a horrifying visage. The hair became scraggily, the skin charred and blistered, the mouth distorted with blackened teeth. Surging forward, it stopped inches from John's face and howled, a scream half fury and half agony.

"Move!" Tom practically dragged Cindy toward the exit.

John emptied his bladder and his bowels. Debbie ran forward, grabbed his arm, and yanked him away. As they chased after the others, Debbie cast a glance over her shoulder, praying the thing wasn't following them. It stood where they had left it, the terrifying look still on its face, its blood-red eyes fixed on her.

The spirit collapsed into a glowing yellow mist that blew away in the wind.

A Thank You to My Readers

Writing and working for the CIA have been two of the most fulfilling things I've done with my life. The best part is having fans who read my books, enjoy them, and want more. I'm extremely fortunate and grateful that I have such a loyal fanbase. You keep reading and I'll keep writing.

If you enjoyed *The Ghosts of Eden Hollow*, please post a review on Amazon and/or Goodreads. It doesn't have to be long—just a rating and a sentence or two about why you liked it. This a new series for me, as well as a new genre; if it's successful, I have plans for several sequels. To be successful in this genre, I need your support. Thank you all in advance.

Acknowledgments

Writing is solitary and lonely. Getting a book published, on the other hand, is a complicated process involving many people, all of whom deserve to be recognized.

A huge debt of gratitude goes to Rhian Lockard. When I started researching the novel, I had little understanding of the paranormal. Rhian spent an hour with me on the phone one evening explaining the reality of spiritual hauntings and spectral cleansings and answering all my questions. The background was instrumental in writing this book. She's been extremely supportive. Any errors in how to perform a cleansing, or any intentional diversions from reality for the sake of literary license (such as allowing spectral images to adopt corporeal form or mentally merging with a living person), are all on me.

A major thanks goes out to my beta readers who have been with me from book one: Michael Atkinson, Pammy Troupe, Tom Williamson, Dan Uebel, Norma Seitz, Roseann Powell, Doc Fried, Paul Semke, and Cari Laffrenier Thompson. They point out grammatical/spelling errors, plot flaws, inconsistencies, and offer their opinion on whether they like the story. I would be lost without them.

Warren Design created the cover art for *The Ghosts of Eden Hollow*. Their work perfectly fits the mood of this book. I'm looking forward to working with them in the future.

As always, a major debt of thanks goes to my family, human and furry. While working at home allows me to set your own hours, for a workaholic like me it means I put in more than forty hours a week. I couldn't do this without their love, patience, and support.

About the Author

Scott M. Baker was born and raised in Everett, Massachusetts and spent twenty-three years in northern Virginia working for the Central Intelligence Agency. Scott is now retired and lives just outside of Concord, New Hampshire with his wife and fellow writer Alison Beightol, stepdaughter, two rambunctious boxers, and two cats who treat him as their human servant. In addition to his paranormal series, he is currently writing the *Nurse Alissa vs. the Zombies* saga, his latest zombie apocalypse series. Previous works include the *Shattered World* series, his five-book young adult post-apocalypse thriller about a group of adventurers attempting to close interdimensional portals into Hell; *The Vampire Hunters* trilogy, about humans fighting the undead in Washington D.C.; *Rotter World, Rotter Nation,* and *Rotter Apocalypse,* his first post-apocalyptic zombie saga; *Yeitso,* his homage to the giant monster movies of the 1950s that he loved watching as a kid; as well as several zombie-themed novellas and anthologies.

Please check out Scott's social media accounts for the latest information on future books, upcoming events, and other fun stuff.

Blog: scottmbakerauthor.blogspot.com
Facebook: facebook.com/groups/397749347486177
Twitter: twitter.com/vampire_hunters
Instagram: instagram.com/scottmbakerwriter